M000195618

Advanced praise for *Char*

"*Charlotte Zielinski, to whom we were first introduced in Julia's Gifts, is a strongly positive role model for our daughters. I would add Charlotte's Honor to the must-read list for any historical fiction, mother-daughter generational, or virtue-based book club. Of course, Gable's tales are perfectly delectable as a personal poolside treat as well!*"
Jean Egolf, author, *the Molly McBride series*

"*Charlotte's Honor includes a little bit of everything: WWI history, sweet romance, and a little mystery/suspense. This page-turning love story (it's a fast read!) is built on a foundation of faith and above all, the dignity of human life. Charlotte's Honor is not only a pleasant romantic escape but edifying as well.*"
Carolyn Astfalk, author, *Ornamental Graces*

"*Set toward the end of the Great War, Charlotte's Honor allows readers to glimpse ugliness and death, blossoming relationships, and the most challenging experiences a person could face, juxtaposing the brutality of war with the beauty of sacrificial love.*"
Theresa Linden, award-winning author of Catholic Fiction

"*A charming story set in WW II France where love and faith endure through times of trial. Though Charlotte must face death every day, her commitment to kindness leads to hope and a new life.*"
A.K. Frailey, author, *Last of Her Kind*

Books by Ellen Gable

Emily's Hope, IPPY Honorable Mention 2006
In Name Only (O'Donovan Family #1) winner, IPPY Gold Medal, 2010
A Subtle Grace (O'Donovan Family #2) finalist, IAN 2015
Stealing Jenny (bestseller with nearly 300,000 downloads on Kindle)
Come My Beloved: Inspiring Stories of Catholic Courtship
Image and Likeness: Literary Reflections on the Theology of the Body
(with Erin McCole Cupp)
Dancing on Friday, The Story of Ida Gravelle

Great War Great Love Series
Julia's Gifts (Book 1)
Ella's Promise (Book 3: coming 2019)

Contributor to:
Word by Word: Slowing Down With The Hail Mary
edited by Sarah Reinhard
Catholic Mom's Prayer Companion
edited by Lisa Hendey and Sarah Reinhard
God Moments II: Recognizing the Fruits of the Holy Spirit
God Moments III: True Love Leads to Life
edited by Michele Bondi Bottesi
*After Miscarriage: A Catholic Woman's Companion to
Healing and Hope* edited by Karen Edmisten

Charlotte's Honor

(Great War Great Love
Book Two)

by Ellen Gable

Full Quiver Publishing
Pakenham, Ontario

This book is a work of fiction. Characters and incidents are products of the author's imagination. Real events, places and characters are used fictitiously.

Charlotte's Honor
(Great War Great Love
Book Two)
Copyright 2018 Ellen Gable

Published by
Full Quiver Publishing
PO Box 244
Pakenham, Ontario K0A 2X0
www.fullquiverpublishing.com

ISBN Number: 978-1-987970-04-3

Printed and bound in the USA
Cover design: James Hrkach, Ellen Hrkach
Cover photo Background: Mikel Martinez de Osaba (Mimadeo)
Model photo: James Hrkach

NATIONAL LIBRARY OF CANADA

CATALOGUING IN PUBLICATION

Published by FQ Publishing
A Division of Innate Productions

Dedicated to the memory
of my maternal grandparents,
John (1896-1969) and Bessie (1898–1967) May,
whose 'Great Love' began during the Great War
and lasted for over 50 years until her death.

"Love will always be victorious. When someone loves, he can do everything." St. Teresa of St. Augustine (Martyr of Compiegne)

"It is not death that will come to fetch me, it is the good God. Death is no phantom, no horrible specter, as presented in pictures. In the catechism it is stated that death is the separation of soul and body, that is all! Well, I am not afraid of a separation which will unite me to the good God forever."
St. Thérèse of Lisieux

"But death replied: 'I choose him.' So he went,
And there was silence in the summer night;
Silence and safety; and the veils of sleep.
Then, far away, the thudding of the guns."
Siegfried Sassoon, "The Death Bed"

Note to Reader:
American spellings are used in Charlotte's sections
and British spellings in Paul's sections.

Chapter One
First Encounter

May 1918
Vauxbuin Field Hospital
Near Soissons, France

The air was thick with the mineral stench of blood. Inside the canvas tent that served as Barrack Number 48, Charlotte searched for a place in the unconscious soldier's body to insert the hypodermic. The poor gentleman had burns and wounds everywhere, but she managed to find a one-inch diameter spot on his thigh in which to plunge the needle. The man didn't flinch, and Charlotte suspected that his injuries were too grave for him to survive. She recited a silent prayer for this man's soul, then moved on to the next soldier.

The large canvas tents that were part of the field hospital covered the lawn in front of the *chateau*. Most volunteers referred to it as a *chateau* because it looked the part with its high ceilings, plentiful rooms and marble floors. However, it wasn't a castle. It was a 19th century country manor.

A tendril of dark brown hair slipped from her headscarf, and she tucked it back in. Charlotte Patricia Zielinski didn't care much whether her unruly hair was tame, but she did care about keeping healthy. She wasn't a large girl, nor was she small. However, roughhousing with her brother Ian for so many years made her strong.

After preparing another soldier for the operating theater, she took a short break and sat on a bench near the tent.

She glanced up at the dark sky, enjoying the quiet. After the sunrise, she'd hear the distant booming that came with being ten miles from the front.

After her bout with influenza last month, she'd felt fatigued for weeks. In the past few days, she had enough energy to move a mountain.

Sister Betty, the medical volunteers' middle-aged supervisor, called to her from the barrack beside her, Number 49. She was a big-boned woman who seemed taller because she always stood so straight. Charlotte wasn't sure whether it was because she was British or because she was a big woman, but she also had a booming personality and a loud voice.

Charlotte stood up to speak with Sister.

"How many more men have to be prepared for the O.R., Miss Zielinski?"

"Four, Sister."

"Maybe you'd be of more use in this barrack." She pointed toward Number 49.

"Certainly." She turned to alert her co-worker in 48, when Sister yelled, "Wait."

Charlotte stopped. "Yes?"

"Perhaps you'd better stay where you are. If there are only four left to prepare, finish that duty, then report to this barrack."

"Yes, ma'am."

It took a bit of getting used to, but here in Europe, nurses were referred to as sisters. And all sisters – and most medical volunteers – wore headscarves that looked like habits.

She approached a soldier on a cot, noticing the maple leaf on his collar. Canadians tended to be an agreeable bunch. He pursed his lips as she stripped his clothes, wincing as bits of skin came off with his pants. The poor fellow tensed, but Charlotte could only offer, "I'm so sorry. I am doing my best not to hurt you."

The dark-haired man attempted a smile.

An ear-piercing explosion caused the world around Charlotte to vanish, and she reflexively collapsed on the cot, falling across the soldier lying in front of her. Ears ringing, she remained still for what seemed like an hour but was likely a few minutes. Blinking, she opened her eyes and stared at the metal side of the cot in front of her and felt the soldier moving underneath her.

As she lifted herself up, not one but three large drops of blood splattered the white sheet below her. Her head seared in a flash of pain.

When the Canadian soldier took hold of her hand, he said something she couldn't hear.

His warbling soon became words. "Are you all right, Miss?"

Her mouth was open, but she couldn't speak. Nodding, she raised her hand to her headscarf. When she pulled her hand to her face, it was covered in blood. *Jesus, Mary, and Joseph.*

"Are...*you* all right, sir?" Charlotte asked the man.

"Yes, no worse than I was. Thanks to you, Miss. You shielded my body with yours." He paused. "You have a bad shrapnel wound on your head."

"Y...yes." Charlotte winced but forced a smile. She turned and picked up a bandage from the side of the overturned cart. She pressed it to her head.

By this time, the entire ward was awake and bustling with moaning soldiers.

Standing up, her surroundings seemed to shift and sway, so she reached for the soldier's hand. "I'm so sorry."

"Think nothing of it. I'm happy to reciprocate."

Glancing just above the soldier's head, she spotted five or six holes the size of watermelons blown through the side of the barrack's canvas wall and hundreds dotting the rest of the walls. Following the holes from the side wall to the ceiling, she stared upwards at the roof of the tent, now shredded in many places.

A few soldiers near the wall had sustained minor injuries, but no one appeared to be mortally wounded.

Panicked and fearing the worst, Charlotte rushed outside, the bandage still to her head. As she turned toward the adjacent barrack, she stopped and gasped. The influenza ward was no longer there. Body parts, blood, torn-apart furniture, and bits and pieces of the barrack were all that remained. The realization that she had escaped death made her knees buckle.

She blessed herself and lowered her head. *"Requiescant in pace."* Her hearing had not yet fully returned, but she could hear someone call her name.

Her friend Julia approached, her eyes wide and worried. "I was so afraid that you were in the barrack that exploded." Julia grabbed her by both elbows.

"I...I was in the...critical care unit." Charlotte paused, as it was difficult to speak. "Got a... pretty nasty cut. I'm ...happy to be alive."

"Thank God. You best get some treatment for that, Charlotte."

"Indeed. Thank God."

Julia scowled in concern. "Do you need help getting to a doctor? You're bleeding quite a bit."

"No, I...should be fine. I can get there on my own." She paused. People were rushing back and forth. Some, like Charlotte, were bleeding from injuries. Stretcher-bearers pushed forward to retrieve the wounded and the dead. Sobs and shouts filled the air. "Besides, I'm sure you're needed elsewhere."

Julia rubbed Charlotte's shoulders, then proceeded to help others who had been injured.

Someone pulled her by the arm and escorted her toward the *chateau*. "Miss Zielinski, come. I'll take you inside to the *chateau*. Some of the nurses and Dr. K are treating the minor wounds."

Her wound was considered minor, but it stung like the dickens, and she needed stitches.

***

Paul jerked awake at the sound of an explosion. He flung the blankets back and tore out of bed, his stomach sinking. He didn't need to see it to know what happened. The field hospital had taken a direct hit. Crossing the room and entering the hallway, he peered out the tall window facing the front and balled his fists. One of the barracks had been destroyed, all its occupants dead. Didn't that blasted Hun Army realize this was a hospital? And that medical staff helped *both* Allied and enemy soldiers? Of course, they did. The giant red cross on the roof of the *chateau* and the barracks attested to that fact.

Paul Alistair Kilgallen, MD, wouldn't have time to shave, so he dressed quickly and glanced in the mirror. His brown wavy hair sprinkled with grey was dishevelled so he ran his fingers through it.

He rushed out to the scene. Since the people in the bombed barrack were certainly dead, the occupants of the barracks on either side likely sustained wounds. Today would be spent first stitching wounds of nurses and assistants, then back to the operating theatre doing his best to save lives.

Paul put his hands on his hips. Sister Betty strode toward him, weaving around two other nurses and a soldier on crutches. "Dr. K, we'll need you inside the *chateau*. We've already gathered a group of young women who need stitches. Most of the injured are our medical aid workers. And we lost two in the barrack that was bombed."

"Sorry to hear that, Sister." He followed Sister Betty to the dining hall.

The first young woman had a small shrapnel wound in her arm, and she sobbed noisily as he stitched it. He fancied her to be the feminine sort who cried at a comedic motion picture.

Next, he approached a young medical aid worker who sat quietly on a chair with her hair covered in a very bloodied headscarf. Judging from the amount of blood, he was surprised the girl hadn't gone unconscious, but then again, head wounds always bled profusely.

"Miss?"

"Yes?"

"Let's see what you have there."

The girl untied the headscarf, so Paul could examine her wound. It was a deep wound that appeared to have some shrapnel left inside. As he examined the laceration, his eyes wandered to the shoulder area of her apron and the girl's brown scapular that sat askew. He had worn a scapular as a child and young adult, but since university when he stopped attending Mass, he had no use for any religious artifacts.

He made eye contact with the girl, and she continued to gaze at him with intense brown eyes. Her cheeks were free of any tears, and Paul could only surmise that she had a high pain tolerance, given the amount of discomfort she must have.

He first cleaned the wound with alcohol.

The girl jerked, muttered, "Son of a –" then drew in a breath. "Sorry, sir. That stung like the dickens."

He admired a girl who didn't hide her feelings. Obviously, she wasn't a crier. After cleaning the wound, he had to pick around to ensure he'd removed all the shrapnel. He was getting impatient with himself. However, the girl remained silent, her lips pursed. She hadn't spoken since the dickens comment.

"Doctor?"

"Yes," he said, looking up.

Sister Betty stood in front of him. "Critical case in the operating theatre, ready for you. He was outside the barrack smoking a cigarette when the bomb hit. His back is shredded with shrapnel."

"That cigarette probably saved his life."

"Well, that'll depend on whether you can get to him quickly."

"Right away."

The girl shrank away from him as he dug one last time and finally picked the metal out.

"Sister?"

Sister Betty stepped forward. "Yes?"

Paul handed her the needle. "This girl is ready to be stitched. The laceration is nearly four centimeters long. Use the higher-grade stitching, if you please."

Turning his attention back to the girl, he was surprised to see her chin lifted, and she was staring at him squarely in the eyes.

"Sister is going to stitch you, Miss..."

"Thank you, sir. When may I get back to work?"

Paul tried to hide a smile. This girl wanted to get back to work immediately? "Light duty for the next two days, Miss..."

"Zielinski. Charlotte Zielinski."

"Miss Zielinski, you likely suffered a concussion as well. If you want to return to active duty at the end of two days, you may."

"Thank you, sir."

***

Later that day, after spending the morning in one of the main floor rooms, Sister Betty reminded Charlotte that she was to rest, even if she wasn't tired. Charlotte asked Sister about the fate of the man in the operating theatre, the one who had been smoking a cigarette when the barrack was bombed. "He survived, thanks to Dr. K."

Charlotte breathed a sigh of relief. Dr. K. was nice, and one might even say he was handsome. Although he had a sprinkling of gray hair, he appeared to be young, perhaps eight to ten years older than Charlotte's twenty-one years. He was friendly, and according to Sister Betty, he was a brilliant surgeon who had already saved many soldiers.

One hand on her aching head, Charlotte climbed the stairs to the dorm where she piled pillows at the head of the cot, then relaxed against them.

Last March, when she saw the sign in Camden that the Allied Forces needed volunteers, it seemed an ideal decision. Her father had died the previous year. Her brother, Ian, declared it was time for him to enlist. Charlotte tried to dissuade him, tried to appeal to his sense of family. After all, he was her only blood relative. But he refused to listen. He kept saying, "I'll be fine. I'm too stubborn to die." And he'd laughed. Within six months, just before Christmas, she received the telegram that he had been killed in action.

She had no idea what she would've done without her faith. In fact, she tried to attend Masses held here at the field hospital. But they were unfortunately few and far between. She did her best to recite the rosary daily and the prayer to her guardian angel every Sunday:

O Holy Angel at my side,
Go to Church for me,
Kneel in my place, at Holy Mass,
Where I desire to be.

At Offertory, in my stead,
Take all I am and own,
And place it as a sacrifice
Upon the Altar Throne.

At Holy Consecration's bell,
Adore with Seraph's love,
My Jesus hidden in the Host,
Come down from Heaven above.

Then pray for those I dearly love,
And those who cause me grief,
That Jesus' Blood may cleanse all hearts,
And suff'ring souls relieve.

And when the priest Communion takes,
Oh, bring my Lord to me,
That His sweet Heart may rest on mine,
And I His temple be.

Pray that this Sacrifice Divine,
May mankind's sins efface;
Then bring me Jesus' blessing home,
The pledge of every grace. Amen

What *was* her purpose in life? Why did every member of her family have to die and leave her? During one particularly melancholic moment while waiting on the train platform back in the States, she wondered what would happen if she just walked onto the train tracks in front of the arriving train. Would anyone grieve *her*? Would anyone even *miss* her?

Of course, she would *never* have done it because suicide was a mortal sin. Besides, she would *never* give in to despair. She obviously had a purpose in life; she just had to figure out what it was.

Truth be told, those in the parish rectory would likely miss her, but Fr. Kowalski would find someone else – someone more qualified – to replace her. He had been so kind to hire her as an assistant after her father died. It didn't pay much, but it was enough to cover the bills and allowed her to remain in the small row house she had always called home.

Although Ian was ten months younger, most of their

growing-up years, they were the same size. He was her pal, her confidant, and her best friend.

Irish twins were what Papa called Charlotte and her brother. She was born in November of 1896, and Ian arrived ten months later. After Ian's birth, Mama was never well again. Charlotte only remembered her as a bedridden woman. Mama passed away when Charlotte was six and Ian, five.

Charlotte's tiny hand held her mother's thin, pale one. The girl wasn't big enough to lift herself onto the bed, so she stood and held her mommy's hand for what seemed like an entire day. The little girl wanted her mommy to get out of bed and be like other mommies: making food, washing clothes and hugging Charlotte when she got hurt. But Mommy was never like that. Soon, the doctor tried to get the little girl to leave but Papa wouldn't let him. "This is no place for a small child, sir. She needs to leave. Your wife is dying."

"She's not leaving."

Charlotte held onto Mommy's hand. Maybe if she held on tightly, Mommy would stay and wouldn't go to heaven.

Papa passed away the year before the war.

***

The day after the explosion, Charlotte was assigned light duty in the basement kitchen, helping prepare and cook food for the day. She liked it – although it was not as interesting as caring for soldiers. But she did as she was told. Her head laceration stung, and she felt a bit faint, so she sat while she peeled potatoes and listened to the chatter of the kitchen workers, mostly women, and from the sound of their delightful accents, Irish and Scottish.

Her favorite moment of the day was when the workers

screamed and pointed at the floor. Below them, a common field mouse was scurrying around. Charlotte laughed. As the women jumped on chairs, Charlotte stood and placed the potatoes and peeler on her chair. The women let out a collective gasp as Charlotte calmly crouched and took hold of the little rodent by the tail. She brought him to the back door. Nudging the door open, she gently placed the mouse down on the grass, where he darted off.

When she returned to the kitchen, she was met with wide stares and frowns. Ignoring them, Charlotte proceeded to the sink and washed her hands thoroughly, thankful for the running water. Finally, the ladies stopped staring and began to speak among themselves once again.

By the weekend, there was a beautiful lull in the fighting and, with it, fewer casualties.

Earlier that day, one of the volunteers shared her experience in the death ward, and the rest of the volunteers gathered around as she told her tale of the moaning, thrashing, and weeping of the dying soldiers. "I hope never to be assigned there again," the girl had said.

Being assigned to the death ward would be difficult. However, Charlotte had been present when both her mother and father had passed. It would certainly be different if the person dying was someone she hadn't known.

While her friends Julia and Ann took a stroll around the grounds, Charlotte caressed her violin, the one her father had given her, the back of which was beautifully decorated with intricate carvings. She searched for an audience and found one in the officers' ward on the second floor.

The three men clapped along with a lively Irish tune. These were the times she was happy she had brought the violin with her. She was not nearly as proficient as Papa, but she was still learning. Ian had always told her that if she cared for him at all, she'd stop playing the violin and take up another instrument. But how could she do that? She wanted to play violin like Papa, and Papa had always encouraged her. "Keep playing, Charli. You'll get it some day." Papa spent five years carving the back of the instrument for her. Having it here in France made her feel close to him.

***

In the eighteen months since Paul had arrived in France, he had become a different man: certainly he was greyer. He held a tight rein on his emotions since showing one's feelings was for the weak, not the strong. And that was just the way he wanted it.

His reflection in the mirror cringed as he finished shaving. What *was* that awful noise?

Paul prided himself on being tolerant. But if that awful scratching that masqueraded as music didn't cease, he would take matters into his own hands.

On edge since he had heard that screeching coming from down the hall, Paul found himself grinding his teeth. It finally stopped. Was that clapping? Surely, anyone who applauded for that atrocious excuse for music was either deaf or – at the very least – tone deaf.

If Paul hadn't gone into medicine, he would have studied music. From a young age, he had played classical violin with "brilliance," according to his teacher. He hadn't had time to pick up the instrument since enlisting last year.

When he told his parents he would be enlisting, their reactions were a mixture of pride and fear for his safety and for carrying on the Kilgallen name. But they seemed to understand his desire to enlist and to escape from the recent turmoil at home. Paul was the oldest and only son of five children of Alistair and Grace Kilgallen. He was raised in a well-to-do neighborhood of Ottawa, Ontario, and attended Ottawa University for his undergraduate degree. He could've stayed there for his medical degree, but at that point in his life, he needed to be in another city, given how much his parents and sisters expected him to be involved with family activities.

He loved his family dearly, but most of his sisters – and some of his brothers-in-law – were chatterboxes. Paul preferred quiet solitude. After attending Queens University in Kingston for his medical studies, he remained in silent solitude at Hotel Dieu Hospital in the same town. His parents didn't need to remind him that all his sisters were married, and he already had ten nieces and nephews, with two more on the way.

Basic training in Ottawa took only six weeks, and Lieutenant Kilgallen, surgeon, set sail for France.

A knock at the door jolted Paul into the present. He opened it to find Major Peter Winslow, a fellow Canadian and one whose hometown, Arnprior, was close to Peter's.

"What can I do for you, Major?"

***

At the request of one of the men, Charlotte put down the violin and played card games with the soldiers. They had just finished a rousing game of "Go Fish" when Sister Betty called her name from the doorway of the officers' quarters.

Charlotte placed her cards on the table and went over to greet the woman. "Hello, Sister."

"Good day. I know this is your day off, but..."

"Yes?"

"I need assistance with a few soldiers."

Charlotte's pulse quickened. "What sort of assistance?"

"I need help with several men who are —"

"Are what?"

Sister gave a pleasant smile. "Dying."

Charlotte stepped back and hesitated before answering. "You mean the death ward?"

"Yes. There are two more nurses who've contracted influenza, and I need someone to read to and console the men, if you can."

"I...well...yes, of course."

"Come with me. If you get there and decide you'd rather not, I'll find someone else. But I wouldn't ask if I didn't think you'd be good at this job."

As she accompanied Sister Betty down the stairs, she thought of the many times before her father died that she spent hours reading his favorite books to him, such as *Frankenstein, The Three Musketeers,* and *The Count of Monte Cristo.* Charlotte had always enjoyed reading novels, but she especially enjoyed reading to Papa. It was important to keep him happy because if he was happy, maybe he could keep living.

She could also keep soldiers happy now and perhaps allow them to live longer. Even those close to death didn't necessarily have to die. Besides, life had a way of bouncing back sometimes. She had heard of cases where an animal on a farm died, but then came back to life.

"Charli, you can't catch me," Ian said, a smile on his face.

Charlotte despised the fact that her brother, even though younger than she, could outrun her. At eleven years of age, she was more inclined to play boy games. She didn't have many dolls, but the ones she had were well-played-with.

She ran after Ian in the alley beside their row home in Camden and suddenly slipped and fell. Her leg felt like it was on fire. Blood flowed from a deep gash in her shin. Instantly, Ian was there, holding her hand. She felt weaker and weaker, but strangely at peace. Ian squeezed her hand, and her eyes popped open.

She learned later that she had slipped on a discarded rope and gouged her leg on a broken bottle as she fell to the ground. After that, Ian never left her side. He always let her win races and played whatever game she wanted. *I miss you, Ian. I miss you, Papa.*

Holding onto her father's hand, Charlotte squeezed, and Papa's eyes opened. "Charli, I love you."

"Love you too, Papa."

"I wish I didn't have to go."

"Then don't. Don't leave Ian and me. Please."

"I...can't...." Papa closed his eyes and his body became still.

Since Charlotte had been present when both her parents had passed, this was definitely a way she could help.

Down at the barrack, Sister Betty held the door open and allowed Charlotte to walk in before her. There was moaning and crying. One man strapped to a cot thrashed back and forth. Charlotte turned to face Sister Betty. "I'm not sure if I can...." Sister Betty had said the men needed calm entertainment, but this barrack was anything but calm and quiet.

"It's difficult, Charlotte. But you will become accustomed to this. You're a strong young woman, stronger than most of the girls here. These men need someone to talk to or to read to them."

"What shall I read?"

"I was able to find an English copy of *Tom Sawyer* and *David Copperfield* in the Soissons Library." Sister held both books out to Charlotte.

"Yes, very well." *The Adventures of Tom Sawyer* was a more suitable story for men in these conditions. She pursed her lips, took hold of the book and crossed to the far side of the barrack where six men were sitting upright in chairs and either moaning or dozing off.

One man — actually, a boy since he looked no older than sixteen or seventeen— gazed at her as if she were the answer to all his problems. His hopeful eyes made her *want* to be the answer to his problems. Charlotte forced a smile and tried to act as naturally as she could. The boy had white blond hair, blue eyes that would've been bright – had he not been dying – and he struggled to take each breath. Bandages covered both arms. *Mustard gas. Oh, the horrible new weapons of war.*

"Good afternoon, gentlemen, my name is Miss Zielinski, and I am going to be reading from *The Adventures of Tom Sawyer* today." She offered them her kindest smile as she sat down.

There was little, if any, response from the other men, but the boy shook his head, and as he tried to take a breath, he asked, "Where?" It was only one word, but Charlotte could tell the boy had a British accent.

"Where what?"

"Where...are..." As he was trying to speak, she touched

his wristband that displayed his name. *Private William Dombrowski.*

"...you...from?"

"Oh, I'm from New Jersey — Camden, to be precise."

"T...tell..."

"Tell?"

He nodded.

"Do you want to hear about life in Camden? It's not all that exciting."

Private William Dombrowski gasped for air, and Charlotte feared he might die at that moment, but he didn't. William nodded and closed his eyes.

"Well, Camden it shall be." Charlotte prattled on for an hour describing shopping and life as she used to know it. She shared with William that her father had worked at the local cigar factory. She talked about her home parish of St. Joseph's. William seemed to hang on every word. In fact, the other conscious men in the group also began to pay attention to her as she told stories of life back in America.

When Sister Betty brought another girl to relieve her three hours later, Charlotte didn't want to leave.

***

Hannah Greene sat on a bench behind the *chateau* and smoked a cigarette. She needed a respite from the backbreaking work. Besides, there were enough volunteers working, and they weren't overrun by wounded at present.

She hadn't wanted to enlist in the medical corps in this godforsaken war. But her great-uncle (and legal guardian) had given her no other choice. He had already arranged for her to marry a man twenty-five years her senior. The elder man seemed nice enough, but when Hannah found out her friend was enlisting, she decided it would be preferable to join the war effort than to marry a man old enough to be her father.

Once she arrived here, however, she had regretted her choice. This was hard labor with few breaks. In retrospect, marrying the older man would've been easier.

Her days were made more pleasant by a certain surgeon, Dr. K – or as she liked to call him – Dr. Tall and Handsome. Hannah was determined to make him her own.

In the two months she had been here, she had been so busy that she found little opportunity to flirt or even make his acquaintance. But she would introduce herself to him – soon.

"Miss Greene?"

Hannah rolled her eyes and turned to find Sister Betty with a pronounced frown and with her hands on her hips.

"You need to let your superior know if you are taking a break. Another girl just came down with influenza and we need you in the critical care unit."

Hannah sighed and stamped out her cigarette on the ground below her. "Right away, Sister."

Chapter Two
Full-Time Honor

Today would be a lengthy day for Paul in the operating theater treating typical war wounds: mustard burns, shrapnel wounds, infections that necessitated amputating limbs.

When he stepped into the surgical room, he set to work immediately. Minutes stretched into hours and with only a few bites to eat during short breaks, he worked non-stop. Miraculously, not one soldier died on his operating table. The only fatalities were the ones who didn't make it to his table.

Not overly idealistic, he did not believe all the soldiers that passed through his care that day would survive the next few weeks, but it gave him some comfort knowing at least they had made it through their surgeries.

His two assistants had left for the evening. Paul had already taken off his mask, gloves, and apron when Sister Betty called to him, "We have one more, Doctor, or he won't make it until morning."

Groaning, Paul almost told her no. But he couldn't – wouldn't – do that. "Yes, bring him ahead." Though his body longed for sleep, he would take one more soldier on, but he had no assistants.

They exchanged a knowing glance.

Sister Betty nodded. "The other nurses have left, so I'll wash up."

***

Every available moment outside of regular shifts, Charlotte spent in what they now designated the death ward. In fact, one evening after a long shift of regular work, then a short shift of reading and telling stories to the soldiers in the death ward, she requested that Sister Betty assign her full-time to help the dying men.

Sister Betty's eyes widened, and she tilted her head. "Most girls ask to work anywhere but there. You want to be there full-time?"

"Yes, Sister. The men enjoy listening to my stories and listening to me read."

"Well, all right. Be forewarned; do not get too emotionally involved. These men are dying."

"How do you know that for certain?"

"Miss Zielinski," Sister Betty boomed, "are you doubting my ability to determine whether a soldier is terminal or not?"

"Uh...no, but if we can keep them interested and happy, maybe they'll pull through. Maybe they don't have to die."

Sister Betty pinched her lips and scowled. "Perhaps this isn't a good idea."

"This is where I need to be, ma'am."

"Men will die, and it is imperative that you *not* become emotionally attached to them. Can you handle that?"

Charlotte straightened her shoulders. "Yes, ma'am, I can."

"Very well. Then I'll find someone to replace you in your usual duties."

"Thank you, Sister." Charlotte turned to walk away.

"And, Miss Zielinski?" Sister Betty held up a chart.

"Yes, Sister?"

"Please refrain from drawing on the charts." Although her voice was firm, it had a lilt to it, as if she was annoyed but not *that* annoyed.

Still, her cheeks warmed. "Sorry, Sister. I do so absent-mindedly." Charlotte didn't remember doodling on the chart. It was a habit she should do her best to break.

***

Another late night in the operating theater. It seemed to Paul that he wouldn't or couldn't ever catch up to the numerous wounded. This evening at least a third of the men were already dead before he could get to them. Nevertheless, he lifted his scalpel and continued.

***

When Charlotte told her friends, Julia and Ann, that she would be working in the death ward permanently, they both gasped. "Dear Charlotte, how could you volunteer to work *there*?" Julia asked.

"It's where I'm meant to be, Julia. I want to make these men's lives as positive and joyful as possible."

"You're a better woman than I," Ann said.

"It's not about being better than anyone, Ann. It's about being where we are called to be so that we can all work together."

***

The next day was quiet with few wounded and no surgeries on the schedule, so Hannah knocked on Dr. K's door. If he was like most men, he would succumb easily to her advances. As she knocked on his office door, her heart pounded as it usually did at the beginning of the chase.

Hannah tapped her foot on the floor as minutes passed. She knocked again.

He finally opened the door. Dr. Tall and Handsome's hair was messy, his half-buttoned shirt and trousers wrinkled. *Did I wake him?*

She smiled as widely as she could. "Good afternoon, Doctor. I'm sorry to disturb you. I wonder if you might assist me."

"Assist you?" Dr. Tall and Handsome had no hint of a smile. In fact, the downward tilt of his lips made him seem annoyed.

"Yes." She stepped into the room, closed the door and stood in front of it. "I have this, um, rash, on my stomach. I wonder if you might examine it."

He cocked an eyebrow. "Miss...."

"Greene, Hannah Greene." Hannah tried to say it in her most sultry voice.

"Yes, Miss Greene, I suggest you take a trip to the doctor in Soissons for an examination. I'm a surgeon and have more important cases to occupy my time. Now, if you will excuse me...." Dr. Tall and Handsome reached toward the door to open it.

Hannah blocked his way. "Ah, but Doctor, forget the rash. Perhaps we could...." She leaned up to kiss him.

Dr. Tall and Handsome stepped back and held her at arm's length. "I'm sorry, Miss Greene. Fraternizing with the volunteers is frowned upon, and I have no intention of getting – involved with any young lady at this time. So, if you don't mind...." He took her by the shoulders and moved her away from the door.

She was in the hallway standing in front of his closed door before she could say anything. *Who does he think he is?*

***

Paul sighed as he closed the door on Miss Greene. This was war, and he realized that some men needed the company of pretty young ladies like Miss Greene. But Paul wasn't looking for or needing the company of any young lady, especially one that was so forthcoming. Besides, he was tired and would've preferred a bit more sleep, given his late night in the operating theatre.

***

Today would be the first full day that Charlotte would spend in the death ward. The regulars were already up and in their chairs in the corner of the barrack when she entered. William's eyes lit up when he noticed her. Charlotte suspected that perhaps the boy liked her and, really, she loved him right back as a younger brother. Because he struggled with each breath, his brief words were heartfelt and powerful.

As Charlotte counted the men around her, she noticed that Sergeant Wilson — Joseph — was not there. She scanned the room but could not see him anywhere.

Corporal Jones, another patient, gave her the solemn news. "Sergeant Wilson passed away at 0400 hours, Miss."

Charlotte bowed her head and whispered, "*Requiescat in pace,* Sergeant Wilson." Sister had told her that men would die. It wasn't her fault – or was it? If she had stayed up all night, if she had stayed with him, maybe he would have had a stronger will to live.

Shaking her head, Charlotte launched into a lively story about her parents getting trapped in the raised arm of the Statue of Liberty during their first year of marriage. She tried to tell it like Papa always told it, and the men — those who could — chuckled, their laughter music to Charlotte's ears.

***

Apart from a few days where Charlotte was needed to prepare men for the operating theatre, she spent her days with the terminally wounded soldiers. She did her best to make them comfortable and happy. One day, while sitting beside William as he slept, she had begun to daydream when she realized she had drawn a flower on William's chart. She tensed and pursed her lips. Sister Betty would not be pleased. Thankfully, she had recently started using a pencil to fill out charts, so she would have to find an eraser – before Sister Betty saw the chart.

Hearing movement, she glanced at the sleeping William to find him awake and looking at her. He pointed to the chart.

"Oh, you want to see what I've drawn?"

He nodded.

"It's nothing, really, just a doodle of a flower."

Well, in truth, it was a mediocre sketch of a flower, but William studied it like it was a Rembrandt painting. *God bless him.*

Chapter Three
Emotionally Involved

June 15, 1918

Charlotte bounced into the death ward late that afternoon, a new novel under her arm. The usual moaning seeped through every corner and crack of the barrack, but Charlotte was now able to block the melancholy noise out, focusing on the men she could help. When she got to the corner where the patients usually gathered, William was not there. She scanned the barrack, her gaze finally falling upon him in his bed. She sighed, relieved.

On her way to his bedside, Sister Betty intercepted her. "May I have a word with you?"

"Of course, Sister."

They walked back toward the door. Sister Betty's shoulders sagged, and she paused before speaking. "William has only a short time left. I told the others that you may want to spend your time with him reading or...."

Charlotte blinked back tears. Then she nodded. "Of course." She waved and smiled to the men in the corner of the room but made her way quickly over to William. He was so still. He couldn't be gone yet, could he? Finally, he blinked his eyes open and opened his mouth to speak.

"Now, now, I'm the one who is supposed to be speaking. Look what I brought to read? I found this in the officers' ward. It's a Sherlock Holmes mystery! I shall begin to read, if you'd like."

For hours, she read to him as he drifted in and out of consciousness. Wanting him to enjoy the story, she even changed voices for the different characters. If he was enjoying the story, maybe he would try harder to stay alive. Maybe...

Finally, William tapped the edge of the cot.

"What is it, William?"

Closing his eyes, he shook his head.

"You don't want me to read any longer? But we must find out who the dastardly culprit is."

He held out his hand. "Hold."

"Of course, I will hold your hand, William." She clasped his hand and leaned close to his face. "You are a beautiful person, William. I'm so sorry you've had to suffer like this." She thought of her brother, Ian. Did he have someone kind to hold his hand when he passed away?

"S...sss...."

"What?"

"S...song."

"You want me to sing?"

He smiled and nodded.

"Well, I'm afraid I only know the words to church hymns. Would that suffice?"

He nodded.

She pursed her lips, thinking of what song she could sing. While she didn't mind singing with the choir back home, she wasn't all that comfortable singing in public. However, her brother and her father had told her that she could sing better than she played violin, so maybe it wouldn't sound too bad.

Charlotte cleared her throat and began to sing quietly.

Let all mortal flesh keep silence,
And with fear and trembling stand;
Ponder nothing earthly minded,
For with blessing in His hand,
Christ our God to earth descending
Comes our homage to demand.

King of kings, yet born of Mary,
As of old on earth He stood,
Lord of lords, in human vesture,
In the body and the blood;
He will give to all the faithful
His own self for heavenly food.

At His feet the six-winged seraph,
Cherubim with sleepless eye,
Veil their faces to the presence,
As with ceaseless voice they cry:
Alleluia, Alleluia.

At the final verse, it felt so natural to look heavenward, so when she sang the last "Alleluia," she glanced down at William and, bless him, he was smiling. She still held his hand, but there was something different about – *Dear Lord.* This was the same sort of expression on her Papa's face when he had died. William was gone. Her eyes became filled with tears, and a lump formed in her throat. She bit her lip to stifle a sob. But she couldn't keep the tears from coming.

Charlotte wept openly and joined the chorus of somber moaning of the mortally wounded.

***

That evening, while Paul finished paperwork in his office, he heard what sounded faintly like nails on a chalkboard. He slammed the papers down and stood up. Whoever was playing the violin again was committing an atrocious sin against music, and it was high time to get to the bottom of it and offer to take the violin off the person's hands...preferably forever.

He followed the wretched screeching to his window and looked down.

A woman in a headscarf – one of the volunteers – was sitting on the ground in an isolated section near the barn, playing the violin against a purple sky. The setting sun sent beams of light through the trees making the scene somewhat picturesque. But that awful noise!

Sigh. There should be a law against people playing musical instruments out of tune.

He hastened to the first floor and stomped out the back door, tilting his head and balling his fists. As he got closer to the barn – and her – she stopped and turned around.

But Paul was unprepared for what happened next. After setting down the violin on the grass, the girl began to weep uncontrollably – and loudly. And he hadn't even insulted her playing. She sobbed, and he did the only thing he could in the circumstance: console her. He assisted her upright and took her in his arms. "There, there. It's going to be all right."

She stepped back. Keeping her head down, she whispered, "I'm sorry."

"No need." *Except for that wretched playing of the violin. I will take an apology for that.* He handed her his handkerchief.

"Thank you."

He recognized the girl; she was the one who had a shrapnel wound after the explosion. Miss – her last name was Polish. First name? Charlene, Charlotte? He had seen her often in the death ward. She may have had a high tolerance for physical pain but obviously a low one for emotional pain. Someone had died, and she'd let herself become too emotionally attached.

"Someone passed away?"

She nodded. "One of the soldiers, William. He was only a boy."

"Yes, I know the one. A brave boy, he was. Now, may I escort you back into the *chateau*? Most of the girls are in their beds and asleep." *Or were, I presume.*

Nodding, she leaned down to retrieve her violin.

He took it from her. "Miss...."

"Zielinski. Charlotte."

"I'd like to have this momentarily." He pointed to the bow she was still holding. "That too, please."

The girl lifted her eyebrows in confusion but handed it to him.

He put it to his neck, tested each note and tuned it. Maybe the girl didn't know how to tune the instrument. Then he played a quiet melody on the violin.

When he stopped playing, her mouth was open, her eyes wide, and her tears now dry.

"Sir, you play more proficiently than my father." Miss Zielinski had an American accent, Eastern perhaps? New York? Philadelphia? "I only wish to be able to play that well someday."

Before he even thought about it, Paul blurted out, "It takes many years of practice. Perhaps I could teach you."

"Oh, no, I wouldn't want to bother you."

"It wouldn't bother me. I haven't actually played since my —"

"Then yes, I would be happy to have you teach me. Thank you, Dr. K."

"You're welcome."

"Thank you also for treating my head wound." She pointed to her head.

"It's my job. No need. Now, let's get you back inside."

***

When they reached the back door of the *chateau*, moths fluttered near the glow of a gas lamp. Charlotte lifted her chin and stared at Dr. K's face. He had kind eyes. He even had a gentle voice. Yes, Charlotte would be pleased to have Dr. K. give her violin lessons. Someday she would play the violin as well as Papa.

"My word, this is beautiful." Dr. K angled the back of the violin toward the light.

"Papa carved it for me. It took him five – very long – years. Especially since I had been waiting for him to finish it. He started making it when I was eight and finished when I was 13. When I finally received it, I didn't want to play it. I just wanted to stare at the intricate design."

"Brilliant, just brilliant. I've never seen any violin this exquisite."

"Indeed, it is. It's the only one of its kind."

***

Paul couldn't stop staring at the violin – or the young

lady. Words could not adequately describe her beauty. Her dark brown eyes, smooth skin, and innocent expression made Paul's heart race.

Shaking his head, he turned his attention back to the violin. Her father had delicately carved acorns and pinecones along the outside ridge of the back of the instrument. In the center was a sparse tree with branches that twisted and turned in varying directions. Tiny cherubs with harps sat perched under the branches.

He glanced down at the girl...Miss Zielinski. He straightened and stepped back. He would not – could not – allow himself to fall in love.

Chapter Four
The Voice of An Angel

June 19, 1918

That morning, Paul was scheduled to assist doctors at the hospital in nearby Soissons. It was a timely change of pace, although war wounds were the same no matter where he was.

In the afternoon, on his way back to the field hospital, he found himself anticipating the evening ahead. He thought about Miss Zielinski, the girl whose violin scratching had put him on edge. Having offered to teach her, they had agreed to meet in the officers' lounge on the second floor of the *chateau* that evening.

His heart began to race before he realized what was happening. He liked this girl. He was attracted to her. Gripping the steering wheel, he shook his head. What in the world was he doing? As much as he knew he shouldn't, he decided to give her one lesson. After that, he would inform her that he didn't have the time to teach her.

***

After her shift, Charlotte opened the drawer of her night table and took out the tiny notebook that had been given to all volunteers upon enlistment. It was ideal for doodling since it came with a pencil. She drew circles and lines with no sense of purpose. Her thoughts turned to William, the boy whose young life was cut short by this horrible war, and she found herself writing his name in the notebook. He deserved to be remembered.

Around six forty-five, she polished the outside of her violin, making sure she painstakingly cleaned inside all the nooks and crannies of the back, then she peered at her reflection in the mirror to make sure she looked presentable. She had little else to wear other than the hospital uniform, but she didn't need to wear her head scarf, nor the apron, if she wasn't on duty.

At five minutes to seven, Charlotte descended the stairs and strolled toward the officers' ward on the second floor. She opened the door and stepped inside. A few officers smoked cigarettes and nodded a hello to her. But Dr. K was nowhere to be seen.

She took a seat by the window and sat for a moment before taking out her violin. Then Charlotte tucked the violin under her chin and held the bow above the strings when she heard, "Don't touch that violin until we've had at least one lesson!"

Charlotte lifted her chin from the violin to see Dr. Paul Kilgallen standing at the doorway with his hands on his hips. She offered him a wide smile, but he did not return the gesture. He joined her by the window.

"Dr. K, thank you so much for offering to teach me."

"It's not completely benevolent, my dear. Your violin playing is – well, quite bad. And it's offending my sense of music appreciation."

"Oh." Charlotte's shoulders drooped. She blinked, her eyes moist, and avoided eye contact. Finally, she glanced at him.

"Look, Miss Zielinski, I'm going to be blunt. I'm not sure that one lesson is going to help you play the violin any better, but I'm willing to try. I just don't have much time for lessons."

"Perhaps we should forget the lessons, sir. If I play as badly as you say –"

"You do."

Charlotte's whole body tensed. Who was *he* to proclaim that she couldn't play the violin? She scowled and with a sharp tone, said, "Well, what makes *you* such an expert on playing the violin, sir?"

***

The girl's reaction was priceless. She truly thought she could play at least passably. "What makes me an expert is that I was considered a prodigy at the age of six. I took violin lessons from the age of four." Paul paused. "Please hand over the instrument, and I'll give you a few pointers, so you can at least play on tune."

The girl held out the violin, which he took. It was out of tune like it was when he had discovered her crying a few days ago, so he tuned it. At least putting the instrument in tune would give her more to work with. When he gave her instruction, she tilted her head and appeared to listen intently. He would tell her which note he was playing and insist that she play it too. Each time she attempted to play the note, it was either pitchy or an unpleasant tone.

"The difficulty, Miss Zielinski, is that there are no frets on a violin. You have to keep practicing in order to know the exact spot to place your bow."

After a few moments, he realized the problem. Miss Zielinski was tone deaf. She had no idea which note was what.

"My dear, I believe you are as close to tone deaf as I've ever heard."

"I'm what?"

"Excuse me, Dr. K?"

Paul glanced up to see one of the other officers addressing him. "Yes?"

"The girl can't be tone deaf. She sings with the voice of an angel. I heard her when I visited one of my men last week in the death ward."

"Really?" Paul doubted it. If the girl couldn't hear pitch well, it was likely she would also be singing out of key.

"Go ahead, Miss. Sing for the doctor," the officer said.

***

Charlotte didn't know what to do. Dr. K wasn't as nice as she had originally thought. He was obnoxious and too self-assured. Well, her singing voice was passable too, but maybe she was also wrong about that.

"Yes, very well." Now, what would she sing?

She stared straight at Dr. K's eyes and began to sing.

Dear Angel, ever at my side
How loving must thou be,
To leave thy home in heaven to guide
A little child like me.

Thy beautiful and shining face
I see not, though so near;
The sweetness of thy soft low voice
I am too deaf to hear.

I cannot feel thee touch my hand
With pressure light and mild,
To check me, as my mother did
When I was but a child.

***

Paul couldn't believe his ears. The girl could, in fact, sing with near perfect pitch and not without pleasant tone. When she finished, he nodded. "I stand corrected. You sing beautifully and quite on tune. Astounding, really. I suggest that you do more singing and cease playing the violin."

When the girl finally lifted her chin, she blinked tears away. Maybe he *had* been a bit too blunt.

Paul had no idea where the idea came from, but he said, "Or perhaps I could accompany you on this remarkable violin as you sing."

Miss Zielinski's eyes widened, and her mouth opened, but she remained silent.

"We would make quite a good team, you and I, for the talent nights here at the field hospital."

"I don't know. Talent nights?"

"Yes, we occasionally have them in the dining hall."

"I've been here three months and have never heard of any talent nights."

Paul tilted his head. *When was the last one? Ah, Christmas.* "I suppose we've been rather busy with wounded. Perhaps we'll have another one soon. And we want to be ready, correct?"

"I suppose so."

By the end of the night, they had practiced three different songs – and no religious hymns. It seemed that the girl only knew the words to religious hymns, so he wrote down the words to "I'm Always Chasing Rainbows" and "Someone is Calling Me," then he taught her the melody of "Home Sweet Home," and she followed along with the

45

words. She picked up the melody and words quickly, so perhaps she did recognize the tune.

How sweet 'til to sit 'neath a fond father's smile
And the caress of a mother to soothe and beguile
Let others delight mid new pleasures to roam
But give me, oh give me, the pleasures of home
Home, home, sweet, sweet home
There's no place like home, oh, there's no place like home

At the end of the fourth verse, she stopped. Her eyes welled with tears. "It's getting late. I should be getting back upstairs to the dormitory."

"Of course. Missing home?"

"No. Missing my family."

Miss Zielinski was young, so she must be homesick. "First time away?"

"Yes, but it's not that. My entire family is gone. My mother died when I was six, my father two years ago, and my brother passed away just after he enlisted last year."

He offered an understanding nod and a gentle tone. "I'm sorry to hear that."

"I was hoping I might be able to visit his grave, but the Army never gave me that information."

Paul's family sometimes posed many challenges, but he couldn't imagine life without his parents, sisters, brothers-in-law, and nieces and nephews. This girl had no one. He fumbled his words. "Perhaps... tomorrow evening at the same time?"

"Yes, I suppose so."

"Good night, Miss Zielinski."

"Good night, Dr. K."

***

Hannah was ascending the staircase when she heard singing and violin music coming from the officers' recreational room. She followed the sound. One of the medical volunteers, Charlotte Zielinski, was singing and – Hannah drew in a breath – Dr. Tall and Handsome was playing the violin. He was actually smiling. Hannah clenched her fists and returned to the staircase. He didn't have time for young ladies? Perhaps Dr. Tall and Handsome has had a change of heart. Hannah planned to make one last attempt with Dr. Tall and Handsome.

***

As she lay in bed in the darkness of the dormitory, Charlotte tossed and turned. She had no idea what to make of her "lessons" with Dr. K. She certainly hadn't expected him to suggest they pair up for talent shows. She still thought Dr. K was rather obnoxious and rude, but if he was willing to accompany her and work with her, she would agree.

She also hadn't expected to share with him that she was all alone in the world. She hadn't even told Julia and Ann. Charlotte wasn't sure why, except she didn't want her new friends to feel sorry for her.

"Home Sweet Home" was a song that she *had* heard before – Papa used to play it on his violin – but that last verse had been too raw for her. The gnawing emptiness that sometimes took over her body when she missed Papa, Mama, and Ian had been overwhelming since she had left Dr. K in the officers' quarters.

She gave into the sadness and quietly sobbed into her pillow. Would the emptiness ever go away?

Chapter Five
Growing Attraction

The next evening Paul had taught Miss Zielinski another song. She had been familiar with this tune, "By the Sea," and Paul hoped that the upbeat melody might prevent her from feeling melancholy again. The girl truly had a lovely voice and a lovely face and demeanor to go with it. Paul would keep things professional. No need to get any more involved than that.

She also seemed to be enjoying the new song because each time she sang it, she became more and more animated, using her hands as she sang.

The officers in the ward also seemed to enjoy her singing and his accompaniment. And truth be told, he had missed playing the violin and had forgotten how much it energized him.

In the middle of teaching her another song, the alarm rang signaling that more wounded had arrived, and each had to retreat to their respective work stations. They bid each other goodbye. Her drooped shoulders told him that she was disappointed their time had been cut short.

Admittedly, he also was chagrined. The scent of her hair, her animated facial expressions and smooth skin – what in the world was he doing?

As he made his way back to the office, he couldn't get her face and her soft voice out of his mind. Even in the operating theatre, momentary thoughts about this girl surfaced amid incisions, repairing wounds, and stitching.

He would have to stop these ridiculous thoughts before they went anywhere.

***

Charlotte raced upstairs to get her headscarf and apron. The time she spent with Dr. K had sped by, and she could hardly believe two hours had passed by the time the alarm warned them that more soldiers were arriving. Dr. K could be brusque, but his dark eyes and his dark hair with streaks of gray made him a most handsome man. She grabbed her apron and headscarf from the rack beside her bed. Pulling the apron's hole over her head, she tied it around her waist. Then she rushed down the stairs as she wrapped the scarf around her head.

Sister Betty met her and a few other volunteers in the foyer. "You two go to the barrack to give hypodermics," she said to a group of girls to the right of Charlotte.

"And you lot," she said, looking directly at Charlotte, "proceed immediately to the barrack to prepare men for the operating theatre."

Once at the barrack, Charlotte set to work immediately, removing clothes from the wounded and cleaning them as best she could. But the men in the death ward – not to mention Dr. K. – were never far from her thoughts.

Chapter Six
Left Behind

July 17, 1918

Today, the sounds of bombing and artillery fire were no longer distant but closer than Charlotte had ever heard them. In fact, if she stood outside the death ward and walked to the west side of the *chateau*, she could see puffs of smoke and fire. *There must be full-scale fighting in nearby Soissons.*

"Evacuate! Evacuate!" Sister Betty's voice thundered behind her.

She ran toward Sister Betty, who stood in the walkway in front of the barracks. "Evacuate? What do you mean evacuate?" Charlotte couldn't imagine trying to evacuate every person – that would be hundreds of workers and hundreds of wounded soldiers.

"The German Army is advancing, and we need to evacuate the field hospital. Immediately!" Sister Betty's voice was firm. "Prepare the men for transport."

Charlotte glanced at the barrack containing the most critically injured and ill men. How would these soldiers survive an evacuation?

"Everyone?" Charlotte knew that they had been close to the front, but this was a field hospital. Why was the enemy advancing?

"Yes, everyone. Now, get going!"

The door of the barracks swung open, and Charlotte turned to see Dr. K. rushing towards Sister Betty. His voice was louder than she had ever heard him speak. "Some of the patients will die if we transport them in a *camion.*"

Sister Betty sounded sympathetic. "I'm sorry, Doctor, but these are orders. We must evacuate."

"Look," he said, "there are at least five other patients who cannot be moved, or they will die. I know because I just operated on them. They are not terminal, but...." He looked around.

With the thought of those men dying, Charlotte blurted out, "Wait! I'll stay."

He turned to her. "What?"

"I will stay. We can move the terminal men and the new surgical patients into a room in the *chateau.*"

Sister Betty said nothing, but Paul shook his head. "They could still die."

"I know, but it would be better than carrying them farther or leaving them in the barracks."

He sighed. "You're correct that someone needs to stay, but I will remain with the men." Paul faced Sister Betty.

Sister Betty scowled, then nodded. "If you insist, Doctor."

"But I *want* to stay. I want to help," Charlotte pleaded.

***

His hands on his hips, Paul stared at Charlotte. He shook his head. "Miss Zielinski – Charlotte – I can get along on my own. Go and evacuate with the others."

"You need help. You won't be able to handle all these men without assistance, will you?"

He didn't have time for arguments. And she was right. He blew out a sigh. "Very well."

The girl looked pleased, her eyes wide, as if he had offered her a shiny piece of jewellery. After all, this was *her* idea.

"What shall I do first?"

Paul spoke rapidly. "We must get these men into the *chateau*. In the basement, there is a storage room off the kitchen. Find whomever you can to move these men, and I will go into the post-op barrack and have the other men moved."

***

The only stretcher-bearers Charlotte could find were already moving patients into *camions*. "Please, I need your assistance," she said to the two men who had just placed a wounded man in the back of the truck.

"I need help moving the men from the death ward to the *chateau*. They can't be transported away from here."

The two stretcher-bearers traded glances with each other and looked ready to say no. Charlotte did what any self-respecting girl would do: she put her hands together as if in prayer and begged. "Please. These men will die if they're taken."

One of the men said, "But they're going to die anyway. What's the point?"

"The point is—" She struggled to push down the rush of indignation, "—that they're human beings deserving of whatever life they have left. And they're not all terminal. Some will die only if moved. Please."

The two men finally nodded and followed Charlotte to the death ward. "You'll be taking the men to the basement room off the kitchen in the *chateau*. Hurry!"

Charlotte assisted two of the soldiers who could walk on their own, James and George, from the death ward to the basement, trying to hurry them along.

One of the men, James, said, "You should've just left us where we were, Miss Charlotte. We're going to die."

"We're all going to die someday, James," was her reply. In honesty, Charlotte hoped James' death wouldn't happen in the *chateau*.

She left James and George in the basement room and was pleased that fifteen cots had already been set up for the men and two extra cots for her and Dr. K. She raced back to the death ward for the two remaining men and found that the stretcher-bearers had already picked one of them up. The man on the stretcher gagged and struggled to lift his head. Charlotte held a basin to his mouth. She called for the only other ambulatory man, Kieran, to come with her. He had suffered from gas poisoning and although he was mobile, he would likely not be able to catch his breath for the short walk across the lawn. In between assisting Kieran and holding the basin near the other soldier's mouth, Charlotte heard her name being called. She looked up to see Julia.

"Charlotte, you're *staying*?"

She nodded. "I can't...leave them. I want to stay."

"But...then what can I do? Can I help you?"

"Actually, yes. I need paper to make notes. Perhaps a notepad or sheets of paper?"

Julia turned toward the foyer then stopped, took something out of her pocket and handed it to Charlotte. It was a small pocket journal with a leaf embossed on it.

"Where did you get this?"

"From a little shop in Philadelphia." Julia had made or bought gifts for her future husband, whom she referred to as her beloved, and this was one of them.

"Oh, no! Julia, isn't this meant for your beloved?"

"It's fine, really. I can always get another one."

Charlotte straightened as stretcher-bearers took the wounded soldier down to the basement. She held the small book in her hands. "This is too beautiful to write in."

"I want you to have it. Please, Charlotte. Accept this gift from me."

Charlotte hugged her tightly. "I shall take good care of it."

"You can do whatever you'd like to it. It's yours now."

"Thank you so much, Julia. Godspeed."

"Godspeed to you, Dr. K, and all the men."

Ten minutes later, all the men who would be remaining behind were safely in the storage room beyond the kitchen. Two cots were already there for Dr. K and Charlotte to sleep, but Charlotte doubted they would sleep much over the next few days.

***

Hannah sat in the *camion*, pressed up against a nurse on her left and a wounded soldier on her right. She watched the field hospital grow smaller and smaller through the smudged back window.

"Can you believe it? Dr. K and Charlotte are staying behind."

"What?"

Hannah turned and listened to the conversation between two volunteers.

"Dr. K and Charlotte are staying."

Those two must have a death wish.

She rolled her eyes. What was Charlotte thinking? Hannah didn't want to die an early death. If both Dr. Tall and Handsome and Charlotte wanted to die, then that was their prerogative, wasn't it? She hated the fact that those two would be together, though, especially since she hadn't yet had an opportunity to see if the good doctor had changed his mind about female involvement.

Chapter Seven
Waiting for the Enemy

Charlotte walked through the eerily quiet cellar of the *chateau*. A few were moaning, and Dr. K was busy treating a patient unable to breathe. The soldier's mouth hung open, and he waved his hands as Dr. K attempted to give him an injection of morphine.

Leaning in close to the man's face, she calmly whispered, "Shhh. It's going to be fine." The man finally settled.

The storage room was less cluttered and cleaner than she had thought it would be. But it was a basement room, so dampness and a musty stench filled the air. There was a small window close to the ceiling on the far side of the 40-by-40 room, which had a large pillar in the center of it. The bottom of the marble staircase that led to the *chateau's* foyer partially blocked off a section of the basement to the right of the door.

The narrow window offered a small amount of light, but the gas lamps that Dr. K had positioned would be adequate for the time being.

Cots were positioned close to each other from the window to the underbelly of the staircase, leaving just enough space so that either she or Dr. K could squeeze in between them. While Dr. K examined patients, Charlotte stepped into the sunny kitchen to search for food provisions.

It was quiet outside with no sounds of the attacking army.

The kitchen workers had taken most of the fresh bread during the evacuation. Charlotte opened and closed cabinets in search of food staples. She found several pitchers and filled them at the sink, then brought them into the cellar. Next, she filled buckets with water and brought a spare one to use as a commode. She had no idea how long they would be in this room and cringed at the thought of having to use a commode in front of Dr. K. But she might not have any alternative.

Opening one cupboard, she found packaged biscuits and soda crackers.

Back in the storage room, Charlotte set the provisions on a table and noticed the journal that Julia had given to her. It was so unique and so, well... nice...that she hoped she wouldn't need to use it.

She placed the commode bucket along the wall behind the underbelly of the staircase. There wouldn't be much privacy, but it was better there than in the middle of the room.

Moaning just behind her made her turn around. One of the resting soldiers stretched his arms toward the ceiling and began to thrash around. "Throat...clos...sing—" was all the man managed to say in a hoarse whisper.

With a tube in his hand, Dr. K. knelt down and suctioned yellow, foul-smelling fluid from the man's lungs, but the poor fellow continued gasping.

"Charlotte, get me a hypodermic from the cart."

"Yes, Doctor." She retrieved the hypodermic and handed it to Dr. K.

"You don't need to call me Doctor," he said, as he injected the needle into the man's thigh.

"Pardon me?"

"If we're going to be stuck in this basement for any period of time, we should be on a first-name basis. My name is Paul."

Charlotte felt herself flush. "Very well...uh...Paul." It felt odd to call the doctor by his first name, but he had been calling her by her Christian name for the past hour.

The soldier finally settled and Dr. K – Paul – turned and sighed.

Since there were no signs of battle yet, Charlotte had an idea. "Do you think it would be all right if I ran upstairs and got my violin?"

With raised eyebrows, he said, "I don't hear any action outside, but it's probably not worth chancing."

"It will give us something to do here and we can play for the men to calm them and we can..." Anxious for him to agree, she waved her arms up and down as she spoke.

"We'll have enough to do with so many critically ill men to take care of, Charlotte."

She crossed the room and with her hands on the sill, stretched her neck and tiptoed so she could peer out the small window. There was no rumbling of vehicles or any noise whatsoever.

"I'm going to chance it." She sprinted over items on the floor, opened the door, and skipped out.

***

With his hands on his hips, Paul sighed but smiled inwardly at the girl's animated nature. He told the truth when he said that he didn't think they would have time to play music, but if it helped her morale to have it with her, then perhaps it made some sense to retrieve it.

***

Charlotte took two steps at a time to the third-floor dormitory and to her cot and pulled the violin case out from under the bed. As she stepped into the hallway outside the dormitory, the rumble of trucks made the ground move beneath her.

Chapter Eight
The Battle of Vauxbuin

Paul was thinking a swear word as he heard the ground move with the rumble of the trucks approaching.

Charlotte, get back here!

Just then, her footfalls sounded on the marble staircase and within a minute, the door swung open, and she burst into the room. He slammed the door shut, watching her catch her breath.

"Charlotte, for crying out loud, what were you doing? Bringing your entire kit bag with you?"

"No, Doctor – uh...Paul. Just my violin and a few other items we may need."

Paul sighed. "We must give morphine immediately to the rest of these men to keep them quiet. Here." He handed her a basket of glass vials and hypodermics. "I've given these three men their shots. You start with the man closest to the window, and we'll work toward each other."

***

Charlotte gave a morphine shot to a man who was semi-conscious. As with many of the men, this soldier's eyes rolled to the top of his eyelids before he closed them again. A good indication the drug was working.

She pushed the plunger of the syringe, injecting morphine into the last man when a deafening boom sounded, and the earth shook. Charlotte used her body to cover her unconscious patient's face as pieces of wood and dust rained down upon them.

Anxiety mounting, she clutched her apron and blew out a series of breaths to gain control.

"Are you all right, Charlotte?" Paul called her name from across the room.

"I'm...fine."

"Sounds like the battle is on."

"Yes."

"Let's make sure their mouths and noses are free of dust and particles."

"Of course."

They examined each man, cleaning their faces, mouths and noses. The sound of more explosions near the *chateau* gave Charlotte the impression that they were purposefully trying to destroy the tent barracks. War was war, but this *was* a field hospital.

Charlotte's heart skipped a beat when she heard Allied planes above. She also hoped there were Allied troops on the ground.

Just then, her bladder signaled for attention. *Blasted extra cup of tea.* She had set up the commode pot behind the staircase to give some semblance of privacy. Thankfully, the noise outside was loud enough to cover any sounds.

***

When Charlotte rushed behind the stairs presumedly to use the commode bucket, Paul gave her privacy by crossing the room to the far side of the cellar. Craning his neck, he peeked outside the window. The remains of a German truck evidently hit with an Allied shell dotted the ground twenty feet from the window of the *chateau*. He heard the hum of the Allied planes above but could see no Allied troops on the ground. A German soldier walked past the window and Paul ducked out of sight. The shadow of another soldier passed by the window. The two men spoke in German, but he had no idea what they were saying.

Chapter Nine
Hidden

The battle raging outside between the Allies and the enemy strangely enough made Charlotte more at ease than the quiet. Explosive sounds meant that a battle was going on. For the time being, Charlotte felt safe, except for the occasional shaking of the ground that loosened materials from the ceiling and scattered them onto the men and cots.

Her stomach rumbled. She took a bite of a biscuit as she surveyed each patient. She hadn't eaten much in the past twenty-four hours, but to keep working, she had to eat. Shoving the rest of the biscuit into her mouth, she watched Paul clean a wound and change a dressing. Before the war, Charlotte would never have been able to eat anything and watch so graphic a procedure. Now, it was all too ordinary.

When she approached one soldier, his unmoving chest indicated that he had succumbed to his injuries and had passed on. Charlotte let out a long sigh and muttered under her breath. She wished she'd known that he was close to death. Then she would have tried to sit with him.

Paul called from the other side of the room. "What?"

"We lost another soldier." She pulled a sheet over the man's head and face.

Paul mumbled something, finished his task, then made his way to the dead soldier's cot. "Help me move him to the outside wall."

"Yes, of course." The two of them lifted the cot and

moved the now-deceased man to the crawlspace across the room. This was one of those times that Charlotte was glad that she was strong, thanks to Ian's roughhousing and treating her as his equal.

Paul faced Charlotte, then stopped and took hold of her hand. "I'm sorry you stayed. You still have your whole life ahead of you."

Touched by his concern, she felt weak in her knees. "As do you, Paul. Besides, this was *my* idea, not yours. I just wish we could've done more to save them. That's why I enlisted. I wanted to help soldiers. I wanted to save men."

Paul didn't respond.

A deafening crash thrust Charlotte into Paul's arms and he fell backward to the floor, breaking her fall, as a wave of dust, glass and pebbles sprayed them from the explosion outside.

When their senses returned, he asked, "Are you all right?"

"I'm fine." Trembling from the shock of it, Charlotte grabbed onto the nearest cot and pulled herself up. Standing and brushing off her clothes, she looked at Paul as he sat on the floor. A superficial laceration marred his face. He held his hand to it and when he pulled it away, it was covered with blood.

"Looks like I've been hit."

"Come," Charlotte said. "I'll clean it up for you." She helped him stand, guided him to a chair near the door, and cleaned the wound. "I don't think it will need stitches." As she finished washing the cut, both remained silent. When she glanced at him, his lips were pursed and his eyes glassy.

Paul scoffed. "Look at us. We're in the middle of a war, a ghastly battle where chemical weapons are burning the skin off soldiers and the insides of their throats and lungs, where limbs are being blown off men's bodies, where shrapnel wounds are making holes inside men's bodies big enough to fit kit bags. I feel so useless."

Charlotte stepped back and stared at Paul. "That's not true. You're saving men's lives. That's your purpose. That's our purpose."

He shook his head. "This damn war. Sometimes I just want to run away. How do you get through the day without joy? Without hope?"

Charlotte cocked her head in response. How *did* she get through each day? Especially those days when the emptiness of losing her family overwhelmed her. The truth was, she did have joy and hope most days, but she had no idea where she'd be without her faith.

"So? Where is the joy?" he asked.

She opened her mouth to speak then closed it again, waiting to formulate her words. Then, almost in reflex, she said, "There is joy, Paul. Joy is in the smile of the man you're taking care of, in the success of an operation. It's in the brilliant blue sky or the rich red poppies on the side of the road. Joy is in laughter and beauty. It's even in the little mice that scurry throughout this *chateau*. You just need to look for it. Where there is life, there is always hope, and there is always joy."

And then, Dr. K – Paul – began to sob, and Charlotte sat down beside him and held him as he cried.

***

Paul straightened and wiped his eyes. He would not appear weak in front of this girl. The truth was, he hadn't cried in years – not one tear since the awful tragedy. Now his emotions were gushing forward. As a man, he was supposed to be the strong one.

Sounds above made his head jerk upward. Thumping and footsteps above meant that soldiers were in the *chateau.* Were they Huns or Allied soldiers? Paul had to assume they were the enemy.

He went to the door to make sure it was locked. Ready to defend the wounded, ready to defend her, he grabbed an axe and stood there.

"What... are you... doing?" Charlotte's voice shook.

"I'll be ready for them when they come in."

"Using... an axe against... men with guns?"

Paul's eyes flicked upwards. Was he that stupid? Or just not thinking clearly. "You're right."

He extinguished the two gas lamps then took her hand and led her to the area underneath the staircase. Because cots had been placed beside the opening under the staircase, it would shield them from any intruders. "If they come, we'll be able to watch them from here and find out whether they are friend or foe."

As he crouched behind Charlotte, he could feel the girl shaking. "Shhh. It will be fine." A foul odor teased his nose, reminding him the commode was directly behind them.

There was a narrow opening between the bottom of the stairs and the cot, so Paul was confident they would be able to remain hidden. That is, unless the enemy decided to investigate the area behind the staircase.

Slamming and crashing noises from the kitchen told Paul that the people inside the *chateau* were the enemy.

The Allies wouldn't be searching an Allied-held hospital.

When the door rattled, Paul felt Charlotte tense and tremble. He rubbed her back and shushed her. Paul's eyes had adjusted to the dark, and with the bit of light from the window, he would probably see anyone coming through the door.

A loud bang sounded on the door, and both of them jumped. He gripped her arm tighter, hoping to provide her with a degree of strength as the banging came again and again.

Lifting his head around the staircase, Paul scanned the critically ill soldiers. All appeared to be quiet. Morphine was a miracle drug in that regard.

After what seemed like several moments of banging, and despite the door being locked, it finally gave way.

Peering through the narrow opening between the cot and the bottom of the stairs, Paul glanced at brown boots and olive-green pants as one man, then another, stomped into the room. They carried long firearms and were definitely Huns.

Paul hoped that the two Germans would leave the critically ill men alone and depart.

The enemy soldiers walked around, picking up charts and vials and leaning over to inspect the unconscious soldiers. That's when one of the Huns came dangerously close to them. The man leaned down to look at the soldier whose cot was directly in front of their hiding place.

Throat constricting and fear thudding in his heart, Paul squeezed Charlotte's shoulders and eased her back toward him.

The man then seemed to notice something on the floor

close to him. The enemy soldier reached over, picked up Charlotte's violin and studied it, turning it around over and over.

Paul felt Charlotte clutching and twisting her apron.

The Hun backed away and said something in German to his comrade, then he tucked the instrument under his arm.

Charlotte drew in a breath, but Paul squeezed her arm to tell her to be quiet. They could *not* get captured. At least *she* could not get captured. The enemy could do worse things to Charlotte than to Paul. If he had been thinking correctly, he should have refused her offer to help. Of course, it was hard to think rationally when he was around her.

The other German lit a cigarette while the one in possession of the violin chatted in German. About what, Paul didn't know.

Just then, more rumbling sounded on the ground above them, then an explosion close to the *chateau.*

Charlotte trembled, and he gently squeezed her shoulders in consolation. With the Hun soldiers still within earshot, they had to be as still and quiet as possible, despite the battle noises outside.

The rumble of tanks thundered above. Another enemy soldier in the kitchen shouted, *Komm schnell*! And the two men left quickly, not bothering to shut the door.

Paul whispered, "I think the Allies might be back." His suspicions proved correct when he heard Allied planes above. Axis and Allied planes sounded quite different, and having been over here so long, it was easy to hear the difference. He found himself hoping that the Allies would win the battle and allow Paul and Charlotte to get out of the cellar. Shellfire and grenade explosions shook the *chateau* whenever they exploded nearby, which was often.

Hours later, the battle continued. Paul had to remind himself to keep breathing. He held Charlotte with the fierceness of a mama bear. The enemy would have to kill him to get to her, and he was prepared, if the Allies lost this battle, to die to protect her.

They said little to each other, but his firm grip on her must have comforted her because she nodded off for a short time, the back of her head resting against his shoulder.

After some time, the explosions stopped. Tilting his head, Paul strained to catch other sounds. Soldiers exchanged gunfire for a few moments longer. Then silence. Was the battle over?

Chapter Ten
Unexpected Affection

Paul waited ten minutes and when no sounds came from above or from the kitchen, he pulled Charlotte out of their hiding place and quickly – but quietly – closed the door.

"What do we do now?" she asked.

"Wait and listen." Not wanting the enemy to see the gaslight coming from the basement, he grabbed the blanket from his cot and draped it over the window. He lit one of the gas lamps.

A soldier roused and moaned. "We only have one more round of morphine. So we should wait to give it to them. We need to think of other ways to calm and soothe them."

"I could sing quietly."

"That may work."

She stood, hands on her hips, a frown sullying her lovely face. "Unfortunately, you won't be able to accompany me on my beautiful, one-of-a-kind violin made by my beloved father."

"Yes, I'm sorry about that, my dear."

Charlotte scoffed. "Just give me one minute with that...."

Paul believed that she would certainly try to do whatever she could to get back the violin. But it was more important that she stay alive and that her virtue stay intact. There's no telling what the Huns would do with her if she were captured.

The girl then crouched between two cots and sang

quietly to calm the now semi-conscious and critically-injured soldiers. Paul was pleased that she occasionally sang one of the new songs he had taught her. She must've been practicing them because she could sing them by heart. Paul, for his part, shushed and tried to calm the mumbling soldier closest to him.

All through the night, it remained quiet outside. Paul didn't know whether he preferred the battle noises that covered up the sounds of the critically ill men or the quiet which meant that there was no battle going on, but any moaning would be heard easily. If any of the men became too noisy, he would have to give them the last bit of morphine. If the siege didn't end soon, there was nothing more he could do.

Paul and Charlotte worked side by side through the night, cleaning mucus from the men's lungs, giving them sips of water and doing their best to keep them calm and quiet. Two more soldiers succumbed to their injuries and died. Four men out of fifteen. It was cool in the basement, but it was also July, and the sickening stench of the decomposing flesh filled the air.

Charlotte sang quietly, almost in a whisper, to the men closest to her. It was uncanny how easily she could calm them with a song. She no longer sang carefree, upbeat tunes; instead she sang religious hymns.

One of the men suddenly called out and thrashed his arms making his cot squeak.

Something overhead thumped.

Paul and Charlotte froze, her wide-eyed gaze connecting with his, his senses kicking into high alert.

Then another thump and footfalls. People were coming into the *chateau*.

Since the door could no longer be locked, Paul threw a chair in front of it.

"Quickly," he said, holding his hand out. Charlotte prepared the hypodermic and handed it to Paul. He gave the moaning man a shot of morphine.

With little sleep and almost no food, Paul's head grew light. He struggled to concentrate and was afraid he might pass out. And yet this girl seemed to have the energy of a dozen men. How did she do it?

A few shots rang out and Paul stopped breathing.

He grabbed her by the arm and pulled her under the stairs. His hands moved protectively around her. Footfalls on the stairs above them made her tremble, and she tilted her head toward him. Murmurs escaped her lips as she shook uncontrollably.

The tapping of the unknown soldiers as they entered the kitchen meant they would be inside the basement within seconds.

Paul did the only thing he could to keep her quiet. He pulled her into an embrace and kissed her on the lips, long and savoring. For a moment, Charlotte stopped trembling and surrendered to the kiss.

The door shook open and Paul pulled away, his head turning toward the door. Charlotte's face was only an inch away from his.

"'ello?"

Charlotte opened her mouth to speak, but Paul quickly put two fingers over her mouth and whispered. "Shh. Could be the enemy."

"I say, it looks like these wounded men were just left here," a man with a British accent said.

"I suppose they couldn't take them when they evacuated. Poor chaps," another Brit said. "Let's get the stretcher-bearers down here to move them upstairs."

Paul breathed a sigh of relief.

"'ello? Anyone else here?"

"They're Allies," he whispered. "Come. We're safe." He felt Charlotte relax. He stood, then assisted Charlotte, and the two emerged from their hiding place.

The siege was finally over.

Chapter Eleven
Reputation Maligned

Sister Betty placed a protective arm around Charlotte as the two walked to a private room in the west wing of the *chateau's* second floor. "This will allow you to sleep in privacy without much distraction."

After Sister Betty left, Charlotte scanned the small room, which was spacious enough for at least six cots. Like other rooms in this *chateau*, the ceiling was high with ornate decorations on it.

A small pitcher and basin sat on a table near the open window, and a warm breeze caressed her face. She dipped her finger and was surprised to find that it was filled with fresh – and warm – water, so she removed her headscarf, splashed her face and washed her hands, then dried them with the towel beside it.

After removing her shoes and apron, Charlotte slipped in between the covers on the cot. The pillow and sheets smelled like fresh air.

The room was far from activity, but the noise and commotion of a *chateau*-turned-hospital created a tense hum. It was perhaps noisier than usual because of the returning personnel and rebuilding of barracks.

So much had happened in the past three days. When Charlotte tried to close her eyes, all she could feel was Paul's lips on hers, the passion and – quite frankly – the awkwardness of it all. She had never been kissed before, so she had nothing with which to compare it. Did it mean anything to Paul? Why had he kissed her? She *had* been on the verge of hysteria. Maybe he'd wanted to calm her. If that was the case, it must have meant nothing to him.

She liked Paul – very much so – and could even see herself married to him. He was handsome and kind. Of course, he could also be blunt and not one for excessive compliments. But when she had consoled him as he wept, she held him with purpose, like when she had held on to men's hands as they died. This was different.

Still, loss of life had a way of affecting one, even if it wasn't one's own life. Maybe after twenty months of being over here, Charlotte would also be sobbing.

And her beloved violin, the one her sweet father spent five years carving? That wretched Hun had taken it, stolen it! Perhaps she couldn't play the violin as well as Paul, but she had brought it here because it meant so much to her.

There was more to think about than her violin. What had just happened in that basement? Did their kiss mean anything to him? It was all so confusing, but her heart was bursting with joy, despite the confusion. What was Paul feeling right now?

***

Paul collapsed on his cot in the *chateau*, oblivious to the movements of soldiers and staff returning. He blew out a long sigh and shook his head.

He shouldn't have kissed Charlotte, but he had no other option to calm her down. Well, that wasn't quite true. He probably could've silenced her in other ways, but kissing her seemed like the right one.

He shouldn't have allowed himself to weep in front of

her. He shouldn't have... well, he couldn't change what had happened. The best thing he could do now was downplay the kiss – and perhaps avoid Charlotte.

***

The Hun opened the door to Charlotte's room and crept up to her cot. He smacked his hand over her mouth.

Charlotte gasped and sat up. *Thank God, it was a dream.* She pressed her palm to her chest to quiet her racing heart. It was dark with no hint of light in the room.

Not sure where the gas lamp was in this strange room, she carefully felt around the floor with her feet to find her shoes and put her apron and headscarf on.

When she was properly attired, Charlotte made her way to the door and cracked it open. A nurse bustled one way down the hallway, while two soldiers strode the other way and rounded the corner. At the far end of the hall, stretcher-bearers carried a patient into a room.

She crept down the hall, nearing the open door of an empty room. Then she heard someone inside the room say her name, and she stopped to listen.

"Imagine Charlotte and Dr. K alone for three days. I wouldn't be surprised if they were involved in licentious behavior."

Charlotte held her hand over her mouth to stifle the gasp. The voice was unmistakable. It was Hannah Greene. Why was she maligning her name? Clenching her fists, she made a decision. She would confront Hannah, but not here. She sprinted past the door and down the stairs. It was time to get back to work.

Chapter Twelve
Awkward Moments

Charlotte stomped down the hall after hearing Hannah's wretched words, but she was determined not to allow that girl to ruin her day. She found herself looking forward to seeing Paul again. It was what was inside him – the selfless and emotional man – that had attracted her. That kiss had to mean something, and it's not often that a man like Paul weeps. For him to trust Charlotte and to openly sob led her to believe that he felt the same about her.

On her way downstairs, Sister Betty called up to her. "Miss Zielinski, you will be taking a few days off. After what you have endured, you must rest."

Charlotte's shoulders sagged. "But...I really do want to be with the men who are dying, Sister. They need me."

"Yes, they do, but if you become ill –"

"Sister, I won't. I need to be there. Please. Maybe I can do something to –"

Sister Betty's mouth pursed into a frown. "Then a short day, my dear. Five hours and you're back in your dorm room. Have I made myself clear?"

"Yes, ma'am, you have. Five hours. Thank you."

"Thank you, Miss Zielinski. I must say, your bravery under fire is an attribute few young women have. I wish there were more like you." The woman paused. "Since most of the barracks have been destroyed, we have been forced to house as many men as we can here in the *chateau.* The death ward is now on the first floor in the dining hall."

"Thank you, Sister."

When Charlotte entered the dining hall, she was immediately greeted with applause from the remaining critically ill – and now conscious – soldiers who had been in the basement with her and Paul.

Smiling, she held her hand up to indicate they should cease their clapping. Her heart burst, though, to see these soldiers conscious and smiling. Most of the time in the basement during the siege, they were drugged with morphine to keep them quiet. How much did they even remember about that time?

As Charlotte read and entertained the soldiers, she thought about Paul. Every muscle in her body longed for more rest, but part of her felt like she had enough energy to move a mountain.

Toward the end of her five-hour shift, the soldiers burst into applause again, and she just about jumped. Turning, she found that Paul had stepped into the dining room. Like her, he waved his hand to tell the men to stop. Then he announced something that Charlotte couldn't hear. He spoke with a nurse for a few minutes.

Wanting to wave or smile at him, Charlotte stood, waiting for him to turn to her.

Instead, without so much of a glance, he hurried out of the room. *He must be busy in the operating theatre.*

She finished her shift, thankful that no one had died that afternoon, and dragged her weary body upstairs to the dorm. On the second floor, before she turned right to go to the third floor, she again saw Paul.

He stood speaking to an officer outside of his office. His gaze flickered to her, but he made no gesture of acknowledgement, not even a smile or wave. So Charlotte walked toward the two men and waited until the officer had finished talking to Paul.

The officer took his leave, and Paul seemed to be forcing a smile. "Ah, Charlotte. Were you able to get some sleep?"

"Uh, yes."

"Good. Lots of work to do."

"Yes."

"Well, good day." He nodded, backed up into his office and closed the door.

Charlotte remained at the door, staring. *What on earth is wrong with him? He's acting like nothing has happened. He's acting like we hadn't just spent the last two and a half days together in an intense, frightening situation.*

She straightened, turned, and walked toward the staircase. Perhaps he couldn't express himself in public. Perhaps they needed to meet in private.

Resolved, Charlotte decided to write him a letter. In it, she would ask him to meet her on the far side of the entrance gate to the field hospital. There was a beautiful copse of trees on that side. They could meet in private near there.

The dormitory was quiet. One girl slept, but the desk near the window was available for Charlotte to use. She opened the drawer to get the tiny notebook to write down the names of the men who passed away in the cellar. Putting it back into the drawer, she spied the beautiful journal that Julia had given to her. She was glad she hadn't yet used it and wanted to keep it that way, as it was too unique to use. She fished around in the desk drawer to find one sheet of paper and an envelope. Promising to replace the paper and envelope, she took one of each out. She took the top off the inkwell, dipped the pen in ink, and began to write.

Dear Paul,

I must say that I felt very awkward with how abrupt you were this afternoon and could only chalk it up to the fact that you would feel more comfortable talking with me if we had privacy.

Therefore, I ask you to meet me at the copse of trees near the entrance gate of the chateau.

I'll be there at noon, barring any unforeseen circumstances.

Truly,

Charlotte

***

After Charlotte had slipped the letter under Paul's office door, she turned to find one of the British stretcher-bearers – was it Harrison? – his hands on his hips and his eyebrows raised, standing near the stairway. She walked toward him and, in an attempt to ignore him, tripped over her own feet. Flustered, she sighed.

"What do we have here, Miss?"

"Nothing. Now, if you don't mind." She moved around the man, but he blocked her from going up the staircase.

It had been busy and noisy since the siege. For some

reason, all was now quiet. She turned and glanced towards the officers' quarters, but the door was closed.

She straightened, chin up and stared at the man.

Reeking of cigarettes and alcohol, a grin stretched across his face from ear to ear. Why hadn't she noticed that scar high on his forehead before?

"Would you please step aside and allow me to return upstairs to the dormitory?"

"Now why would I do that?" He smirked.

Charlotte lifted her chin. "Well, if I call out, then I'm sure I will wake the entire *chateau*, most especially Dr. K, who is likely in the operating theatre or in his office through that door."

"Most likely in the theatre. But I don't mean you harm, Miss Charlotte. I just thought we could have a little fun, you and me."

"I'm not interested in any fun you might want to have."

"No? You seem interested in having fun with the good doctor, no?"

Charlotte bit her lip to remain silent. Finally, she said, "Sir, I assure you that Dr. K and myself have nothing but the utmost respect for one another. Something that you, sir, seem to lack at this moment. Now, please step aside." Charlotte shoved her way around the man and proceeded up the stairs.

Behind her, she could hear the man whispering under his breath, "Not good enough for you, eh?"

***

Sitting at his desk, Paul jotted down a notation on the last chart, then placed it in the "to file" box. He stood and turned to leave when he saw an envelope on the floor by the door. On the front, written in feminine script was "Dr. Kilgallen." He tensed.

He opened it and sighed. Charlotte wasn't going to let him forget the kiss. Shoulders sagging, he knew what he would have to do.

The girl was sweet, funny, pretty – it didn't matter. He couldn't – wouldn't allow himself to lose control of his emotions.

His sisters had already given his parents many grandchildren. They wouldn't care if he never married. Well, except perhaps that the Kilgallen name would end with him.

Perhaps he could write Charlotte a cordial letter and let her know that the kiss meant nothing. Of course, that would be a lie. It meant a great deal to him. But he just couldn't get involved. Yes, a face-to-face encounter would be preferable. Awkward, challenging, and difficult, but that's what he would do. He would meet her and tell her they couldn't continue what he had started in the *chateau* basement.

Chapter Thirteen
Unexpected Encounter

Charlotte counted the hours and minutes until she would meet Paul near the entrance gate. Since there were no new incoming wounded, at ten minutes to noon, she decided to take her lunch break and approached Sister Betty.

"I'm going for my lunch break, Sister. I will return in about half an hour."

"But Sergeant Kennedy is close to death."

Oh dear. How did she miss that Sergeant Kennedy was close to death? Had she become so focused on herself that she couldn't think of others? Charlotte would stay with the sergeant. She could meet with Paul at a later time.

"Yes, yes, of course. I will postpone my walk."

***

At noon, Paul released an exasperated sigh. The girl was unpredictable. After all this, she hadn't come. Well, he would give her ten minutes and that was all.

***

Charlotte held Sergeant Kennedy's hand, humming a quiet tune as he tossed and turned. This poor man had been living his life in battle but had become another statistic, a commodity in the service of war. He deserved to have someone who loved and cared for him as he breathed his last breath. She continued humming and shushing and telling him he was loved. Then he was still.

Charlotte blinked her eyes to keep from crying and

kissed the man's hand before placing it beside him. She covered his face with a blanket and said a prayer for his soul.

As she pondered this man's life and death, she gasped. "I forgot about meeting Paul!" She glanced at the timepiece on her apron. It was 1:20 and she was over an hour late. Would he still be there?

Rushing out to the copse of trees by the gate, she arrived out of breath and with no sign of Paul. She sighed, then made her way back to the *chateau*. She passed a group of men setting up new barrack tents. A man called her name. She turned to see Paul beckoning her towards him. His lips were pinched together, and his eyebrows were lifted in the slightest of frowns.

"Paul, I'm so sorry. A soldier was close to death and I couldn't leave."

His expression softened. "It's all right." He glanced at his feet and sucked in a breath. Then he lifted his gaze to hers. "About yesterday. I'm sorry if I came across in an abrupt manner. But we really should remain on professional terms. You understand, don't you?"

She opened her mouth, but no words came out. *What is he saying?*

Paul continued. "We were in the middle of a very stressful situation, and it's sometimes natural to react emotionally. It didn't mean anything, really."

Finally, understanding what he was trying to say, Charlotte, anger flooding her voice, said, "You sound like you are trying to convince *yourself*, Paul."

He glanced off in the distance behind her, as if worried someone might see them. "It's not like that, Charlotte. It would be wrong to get involved when we have no idea where we will be a few months from now and how much longer this war will last."

Hands to her hips, Charlotte glared at him. "For a short time, I thought you actually cared for me – playing the violin while I sang, laughing at my jokes, and then there's the..." She leaned close to him and whispered, "...kiss."

She stopped, waiting for him to say something.

He stared at the ground.

When he didn't say anything, she continued. "You're right that we're in the middle of war. People are dying horrible deaths, we're tired all the time and hungry for real food most of the time. And we have an opportunity to experience companionship, maybe even love –"

Paul cut her off. "We cannot fall in love, Charlotte, if you're looking for that."

Charlotte's eyes became moist.

His tone mellowed. "Look, you're pretty, smart, kind, and generous. You're even interesting but...." His lips were pinched, and he sighed. "This is war. We have no business –" He scratched the back of his neck. "Oh, never mind. I must go." He rushed off.

Charlotte was left standing in front of the *chateau*. She kicked the grass at her feet and picked up a stone. She wanted to throw it at him, but she changed her mind. That certainly wouldn't be professional.

She turned toward the entrance. She wasn't tired, was pretty sure she couldn't sleep, so she headed to the death ward since she'd be more use there than in her bed.

Whether Charlotte liked it or not, she had fallen in love with Dr. Paul Kilgallen. While she had romantic notions of a knight in shining armor, she was also a realist. Dr. Paul Kilgallen did not want to "fall in love." Besides, if she kept thinking of Paul, she wouldn't be able to focus on the men who needed her most right now.

Chapter Fourteen
Too Many Distractions

Paul tossed and turned all night and could not drift off to sleep, no matter how many imaginary sheep he counted. He hadn't wanted to be abrupt with Charlotte, but he had made a promise to himself years ago. Romance during wartime was a bad idea, to be sure, but it wasn't his primary reason for not wanting to pursue an intimate relationship.

He was fortunate to have a private bedroom off the operating theatre in the *chateau*. It was convenient in case casualties were brought in during the night. Having private quarters made it easier to get a few hours of rest – usually.

Charlotte would forget him soon enough. He suspected from the way she gazed at him that she was already falling in love. Perhaps his curt manner was just what she needed to make her dislike him.

Finally, Paul flung the covers back and got out of bed to visit the dining area to see if there might be anything to eat. He wasn't hungry but hadn't eaten much in the past twenty-four hours.

Downstairs in the dining hall, it was eerily quiet, save for a few soldiers smoking cigarettes and talking. He picked up a stale croissant. Before he took a bite, he heard a distant and sweet voice – it sounded a lot like Charlotte – singing "Somewhere a Voice is Calling."

Paul sauntered to the far side of the dining hall that ran adjacent to what was temporarily being used as the death ward and stood out of view as he watched Charlotte hold a soldier's hand and sing quietly.

Dusk and the shadows falling
O'er land and sea;
Somewhere a voice is calling,
Calling for me.

Dearest, my heart is dreaming,
Dreaming of you.
Somewhere a voice is calling,
Calling for me,
Calling for me.

She finally released the soldier's hand, then placed the blanket over his head. She stood and wiped her eyes. *Poor girl.* Charlotte was a strong young woman and unique in many ways. He wouldn't be surprised to discover that she had been a rough-and-tumble sort of girl when she was younger.

Another soldier closer to the door beckoned her, and the two began a whispered conversation. Paul could hear every other word, then Charlotte stood and walked toward the door. He backed away, so she wouldn't see him. When he heard her speak, he peeked around the door. She read aloud from a book, her voice as smooth as silk. She could probably read the telephone directory and make it sound enticing.

He stepped away, finished his croissant, and returned to his office upstairs.

***

When Charlotte finished reading three chapters of *Moby Dick* aloud, the poor man had finally fallen asleep. This soldier wasn't on death's door – not yet anyway. The man had breathing problems caused by burns from mustard gas in his esophagus and lungs that necessitated treatments three times a day. It was a wonder that anyone with burns in his throat and esophagus could sleep at all. Thank heaven for morphine. At least it was making this man's last month of life tolerable.

Chapter Fifteen
Avoiding the Situation

For the next week, Charlotte tried her best to focus on the responsibilities at hand. But she found it difficult to stop thinking about Paul.

Toward the end of her late evening shift, she carried a box of clean bandages to the supply closet in the *chateau*. Stepping into the small room, she clicked on the overhead light. She placed the box on an upper shelf, climbed onto the step stool, opened the box and began stacking the bandages on the top shelf.

When she was a little girl, whenever someone was mean to her, Papa told her it was because they were hurting inside. Paul was hurting, and she would have to be patient. *Please, God, watch over Paul. Bless him and help him overcome whatever is making him hurt.*

Hannah must be hurting too if she was spreading false rumors about her. She slapped the bandages, shoving them deeper on the shelf as she thought about the girl who was making things more difficult each day. Charlotte wanted to give that girl a piece of her mind. Instead, she prayed for her. *Please, God, watch over Hannah too. Help her to be nicer.*

In the death ward that day, Charlotte held the hand of another too-young soldier and sang him into eternity. *Another name to be added to my book of soldiers.* As much as she wished it might, it didn't get any easier. And no matter what she did, soldiers still died.

Never far from her thoughts, especially as soldiers were dying, was her dear brother, Ian. She prayed that a sweet girl had held his hand as he breathed his last breath. She cleared her throat to rid herself of the lump and squeezed her eyes shut to stop the tears from flowing.

She finished her task, switched the light off, then exited the supply room. It was two a.m. Her shift was over, but she was anxious to return to the death ward in the dining hall. She raced down the stairs when she bumped into someone. Looking up, they both gasped.

One hand on the railing, Paul stepped back, gaining a respectable distance between them. "Charlotte. Why aren't you in bed?"

"Death doesn't keep banker's hours, Paul. I should go." She took another step down.

"Wait."

She turned, her hand on her hip. "Yes?"

"Look, I'm sorry if I was abrupt with you the other day."

"And?"

He stuttered and stammered. "Well, I...."

"And?"

"You deserve someone who won't hurt you."

"What makes you think you'll hurt me?"

"That's what love does, Charlotte. I don't want to hurt you. You've been abandoned by enough people in your life."

"What people have abandoned me?"

"Your mother, father, brother."

"But they didn't...." Charlotte stopped. Paul was right. Thinking back, at only six years of age, she had felt abandoned when her mother died. But the others? It certainly wasn't *their* fault they died.

***

Charlotte came back up the step and closed the distance between them. She took hold of his hand and whispered, "Love does hurt, Paul."

"What?"

"Love is beautiful, but it's supposed to hurt. When we love, truly love another person, we make sacrifices."

Paul avoided eye contact. Her hand was small and soft inside his. He glanced up, down and behind him to make sure no one was around. He whispered, "I don't want to hurt you."

Charlotte squeezed his hand. "I will likely take a lunch break around noon. Let's meet out by the front gate. There's a forest nearby. It will give us privacy."

Releasing a sigh, he nodded. He should say no. He should be firm. He should do a lot of things. But this girl.... "Yes, all right. You may be waiting a while. I have a full surgical schedule in the morning, but I'll take a half hour break around noon."

"Perfect, Doctor." She winked before descending the staircase.

In his heart, this felt right. And his heart certainly wanted it. But in his head, it was wrong. Loving someone certainly did mean sacrifice and pain. He knew that all too well.

He couldn't – wouldn't be able to – stand it if he let himself fall in love with her or – worse yet– for her to fall in love with him and have something happen to him. He must protect her from that.

To do so, he would keep their friendship pleasant and cordial. They would spend a few days together and enjoy each other's presence. Besides, when the war ended, they might never see each other again.

Chapter Sixteen
Nothing Cordial About It

Late July brought the warmest weather of the summer, and Charlotte thanked God for the lull in fighting. In the previous week, Charlotte and Paul had an opportunity to meet by the gate once. She couldn't wait until after dinner when they had agreed to meet each other again.

She understood the need for propriety. Medical volunteers and doctors were not supposed to be "fraternizing." Most soldiers and volunteers didn't obey the rules. After all, it was wartime and anything that improved morale could be a good thing.

They had already shared stories of their respective childhoods – his in Ottawa, Canada, and hers in Camden, New Jersey. He told her his family was well-to-do. She told him her family had been on the verge of poverty most of her life. He spoke about being a musical prodigy and how he'd broken his music tutor's heart when he decided to be a doctor. Interestingly, they hadn't kissed again – and Charlotte was not going to initiate any physical affection.

Charlotte skipped dinner because she had consumed a bowl of stew earlier this afternoon and was not hungry. Besides, she wanted to arrive early for their meeting.

She reached the small clearing by the copse of trees. The warm breeze made the bright green leaves on the oak and maple trees flutter. Charlotte breathed in deeply of the scent of earth and summer. Despite the shade of the forest trees, sweat gathered on her neck.

She looked heavenward at the vibrant blue sky. The grass rustled behind her, and her heart raced.

Turning, she drew in a breath.

"Ah, what do we have here?" It was that Hannah, hands on her hips, a wide smile stretching from ear to ear.

"Whatever do you mean?"

"Waiting for someone?"

When Charlotte didn't answer, Hannah lifted her chin. "Waiting for Dr. K, I presume?"

"What is your problem, Hannah?"

"My *problem* is that war doesn't give us permission to have loose morals."

"What is that supposed to mean?"

"We all know you were with Dr. K – alone – in the basement of the *chateau* for days."

"We were taking care of terminally ill men."

"If that's what you'd like to call it."

"Well, I had come out here to be alone, and I'm not interested in sharing your company, so I will bid you *adieu*." She turned away from Hannah.

Charlotte glanced in the direction of the *chateau*. Paul was just coming down the steps. She immediately turned away and walked to the rear of the *chateau,* hoping that Paul would see her – and Hannah – and not venture towards her.

But it was too late. Paul had seen her – and Hannah – and approached Charlotte at the side of the *chateau*. She glanced back at Hannah and saw that the girl was smiling, her chin lifted.

Paul stopped at a respectable distance from Charlotte and squinted over her shoulder in the direction of Hannah. "What's going on, Charlotte?"

"Hannah Greene is spreading rumors about me – about you – about us. For some reason, she does not like me and wishes to ruin my reputation."

"Then I shall have a talk with her." Paul turned but Charlotte grabbed his arm.

"No, please, don't. It will just make things worse. Can we meet at another place? On another day?"

Paul stepped back, his hands on his hips. "Yes, in fact, I know of an ideal place tucked away at the edge of the forest behind the *chateau*. It's an old stone building I discovered there. Come, I'll take you there."

"We should wait until Hannah has gone."

"Yes." He glanced towards Hannah. "It doesn't appear she is planning to leave. Are you sure you don't wish for me to have a word with her?"

"Quite sure."

***

Charlotte's disappointed expression made Paul want to give Hannah Greene a piece of his mind. But he also respected Charlotte's wishes. And all the more reason they needed to keep their friendship private.

"I better go," she said, gazing up at him like a lost – and very sad – puppy.

"Yes, all right." He leaned close and whispered, "Tomorrow morning at five a.m. we'll meet in the foyer, and I'll take you to the stone building, so you'll know where it is."

"Very well." Two female volunteers passed them. She nodded toward Paul. "Goodbye, Dr. K."

"Goodbye, Miss Zielinski."

***

Upstairs in the dorm room, Charlotte buried her face in her pillow, then pounded her fists against her cot. What in the world was wrong with that girl? And why was she trying to make Charlotte's life so difficult? Wasn't war difficult enough?

Julia and Ann entered the dorm and after greeting Charlotte, began chatting nearby. She wanted to tell them to be quiet, but this wasn't their fault. Instead, she made the conscious effort to join the girls and tried to forget her disappointment.

***

Charlotte woke before the alarm went off. It would soon be daybreak, and the sun would rise in half an hour. She couldn't stop shaking and almost felt as if she was part of some covert spy operation. She dressed as quietly as possible and crept down the staircase to the foyer.

At the bottom of the steps was the figure of a man. Her heart skipped a beat. Paul was already there! She reached the bottom of the steps, and he took her hand and led her out through the front doors and to the back of the *chateau* and the forest.

"We could've used the back-basement door," he whispered. "But we'd have to go through the kitchen. Don't want to disturb the cooks."

Squeezing her hand, he nearly sprinted along the dirt

pathway that followed the edge of the forest. To the right, the tip of the sun was making its debut above the horizon. Still, she couldn't see much but trusted that Paul knew where he was going.

After a few moments, Paul stopped at a small clearing and as the sun rose, the outline of what appeared to be a small structure took shape. About ten feet away from the ancient stone structure, an oak tree sprouted up amidst rocks, its branches like hands reaching for the sky.

Further beyond the tree and stone structure, the ruins of another old building interrupted the grass. Piles of stones were everywhere, perhaps from the ruins of the old building.

Charlotte gazed at the structure closest to them. A wooden cross rose above the arched entryway, which was covered with stones that had been roughly hewn into blocks.

This was most definitely a sacred place. It resembled a tiny church, though it wouldn't be big enough to fit more than ten or so small adults or children.

"This is beautiful, Paul."

"It is, isn't it?" He paused. "It's a medieval building, probably used as a shed or milk house hundreds of years ago. Villagers likely added the cross later to make it a place of prayer. And you'll see that the entranceway has been blocked to keep vermin out of it."

"Do you come here often, Paul?"

"No. I wish I could. I don't have enough time."

"Maybe to pray?"

He scoffed. "Certainly not to pray."

"Why not? It's an ideal place to talk to God. In fact, I'm

wondering why they've never had a Mass out here."

"They've likely never had a Mass here because the Army chaplain probably doesn't know this little clearing exists. As you can see, it's quite a distance from the rear of the *chateau*." He paused. "I only discovered it a few months ago when I was taking a walk."

"Why don't you pray, Paul?"

"Haven't had any reason to, Charlotte."

***

He didn't like where the conversation was going. Turning, he pointed to the bottom of the well where an etching proclaimed the year. "Look. 1402. Judging from the tin roof, it's probably had numerous additions since then."

"Fascinating," her voice came from behind him.

He was staring at the etching when he felt Charlotte's fingertips on his back. He turned, and she took hold of his hand. He stepped back, releasing her hand.

She sighed. "Paul, what are we doing here?"

"I don't know."

The sun rose above the thick brush and sunbeams fell on them, blinding him for a second. Unwilling to turn away from her, he blinked until his vision cleared. Sunlight illuminated her pale skin and made flyaway strands of her brown hair glow.

Charlotte stepped toward him and took hold of his hand. "It's too late, Paul. I love you. And I'm willing to wait until you love me."

What was he supposed to say? *Sure, I'll give you my heart. Heck, I'll marry you right now?* "Charlotte, it certainly isn't for lack of affection for you. I like you. Very much, in fact. It's just that I made a promise...."

"What sort of promise?"

"Look, Charlotte. I'm sorry. I should've told you."

"There's...."

"There's what?"

He didn't want to say the words. He didn't even want to think about...it. He stared at the ground.

"Paul?"

Lifting his chin, he sighed. "There's...someone else."

Chapter Seventeen
Unexpected Departure

She gasped. "You're...you're...married?" Charlotte's mouth remained open, but she fell silent.

He said the words, clear and concise. "Engaged." He lifted his chin. Charlotte lowered her head, and her shoulders sagged, as if he just told her that someone had died. That wasn't far off the mark.

When she lifted her head, tears filled her eyes, but she straightened. "I see." She turned to walk away, but he grasped onto her arm.

"Her name...was Catherine. She was...killed as the result of an accident two days before our wedding."

Charlotte turned to face him. "Oh, Paul, I'm so, so sorry."

Yes, Paul was sorry too. He blinked the tears away. No, he couldn't reciprocate this sweet girl's love. He couldn't share his heart with her. Love was too painful.

But, gazing at her innocent face full of concern and remembering what love *had* meant, he couldn't help himself. He leaned down and kissed her forehead. So much for a cordial friendship.

***

Over the next few days, Charlotte was only able to meet with Paul once. She hadn't planned on expressing her love for him at the stone chapel. She didn't care that he didn't reciprocate. Paul would, someday. Perhaps once he finished grieving, then he could open his heart to her.

Despite long days in the death ward and despite the news that Paul's fiancée had passed away, Charlotte was so happy that she thought her heart would burst. Everything seemed intense: the blue of the sky, the green of the grass – even food tasted better. And to top it off, not one soldier had died in the past few days. She was obviously doing something right. The outside barracks were now rebuilt, and they had assigned the small barrack closest to the *chateau* as the death ward. She was happy to remain close to the *chateau* since it meant she could more easily make it to their meeting place at the stone chapel.

Julia and Ann had asked if she'd like to visit Soissons that morning, but she had said no. An Aussie soldier was close to death, and she didn't want to leave him. She had brought Julia's journal down to the ward because she was planning to give it back to Julia. But mid-day, she had an opportunity to speak with Julia's friend, Major Winslow, who was a Canadian soldier. Charlotte decided to give him the journal. The miracle was that Charlotte hadn't doodled in it. It was all worth it, though. The expression on Major Winslow's face when he saw the maple leaf! Of course, Julia was surprised to find out that Charlotte had given one of her beloved's gifts to him.

Charlotte wanted to believe that she had her own beloved, and some people already suspected, but Sister Betty wouldn't be impressed if they shared anything openly. Of course, she wasn't sure that Paul *was* her beloved. She certainly understood why he acted the way he did. He had loved and lost, and it was too painful. In Charlotte's mind, loving and having that love taken away would be better than never loving at all. And right now, she loved Paul with all her heart.

***

Paul finished a long day in the operating theatre, trying to patch up a casualty clearing station medic's hatchet job on two soldiers. Where did these alleged medics receive their training? The local butcher shop? Was it not common sense that they were supposed to make the surgeon's jobs easier, not more difficult? He had complained to the upper command medical corps that the lack of medical training for medics had caused too many deaths. He cleaned up and went to his office to find "New Orders" sitting on his desk.

Scanning the paper in front of him, Paul discovered that the upper command agreed with him that the inexperienced medics on the frontlines needed more expertise than they had. They were transferring Paul to the clearing station at the front on the other side of Soissons. Sighing, he knew what this meant. A few months previous, when he had mentioned the medic mistakes he had to repair, he suspected they might transfer him to the front. But that was before – Charlotte.

He was scheduled to leave at 0900 hours. Another surgeon would be arriving here around that time. Paul and Charlotte had planned to meet at the stone building at 0500 hours. Should he still go? Paul nodded, knowing he had to obey orders, even if it meant this would be the last time he saw Charlotte.

***

Near the stone chapel, Charlotte paced. At this time of morning, she expected to see a rich sapphire blue sky overhead, not the dark foreboding shade that indicated the sun had no intention of rising. It would likely be an overcast day. Even this brought joy, though. The leaves rustled in the warm wind, and the air smelled of grass. Hurried footfalls rose above the peaceful morning sounds, and then a figure appeared in the distance jogging toward her. *Paul.*

They embraced, and he stepped back. "I'm... sorry I'm late, Charlotte. Too much to do." His voice cracked.

She couldn't see his face clearly. "Is something wrong?"

"Everything is wrong in war, Charlotte."

"Yes, I suppose so."

"I'm also sorry I can't stay very long, but...."

"That's all right." She inched closer and fell against his chest. He put his arms around her. With her head on his chest, she could hear his heart racing. Charlotte smiled at the knowledge that she had that effect on him, even if he hadn't yet proclaimed his love for her.

He patted her back. "I need to go."

"Yes, yes, of course. I love you, Paul."

"Charlotte."

"Yes?"

"We cannot meet any longer."

Charlotte tensed. "Paul, please."

"I'm being transferred to the front. But I had already made up my mind. We cannot see each other anymore. I wish you all the best...and a happy life."

Without waiting for a response, Paul was gone, leaving her beside the stone structure under the dark morning sky.

***

Charlotte returned to the dormitory in the *chateau* but

hadn't remembered walking there. The entire day unfolded in a blur. She was certain that Paul felt some sort of affection for her. Of course, her stubborn nature wouldn't allow Paul to stop seeing her. Taking matters into her own hands, she decided to visit him in his office when she was on break. Certainly, he couldn't be gone *yet*. He might be angry, but she didn't care.

She knocked and a strange middle-aged man, tall and broad shouldered, with a moustache, answered the door.

"Is Dr. Kilgallen here?"

"No, I'm sorry, he's been transferred to the front. I'm Dr. Fraser."

She lowered her head. The man's voice became a jumble of words.

"Miss?"

Looking up, she said, "Yes?"

"May I help you?"

"No, no, thank you, sir. Sorry to have bothered you."

"No bother at all."

***

On her way back to the *chateau*, Julia stopped her. "Charlotte, what's wrong?"

She pressed her lips together, so she wouldn't cry.

"Did another soldier die?"

A soldier had died, but with the emotional turmoil surrounding Paul's departure, the mere mention of it unleashed her sorrow.

Julia embraced her. "There, there, Charlotte. The important thing is that you were there for him."

Stepping back, she nodded and wiped her eyes. "Yes, I know."

"You can always ask Sister Betty to transfer you to another barrack if it's become too difficult for you."

"No, no, I don't want to do that."

In the dormitory, she lay awake staring at the gray ceiling. She got up, pounded her pillow, and slammed it onto the cot. How dare he? And going to the front? Why didn't he tell her before the actual day he left? Surely, he had to have known.

Charlotte's anger turned to sadness as she sobbed quietly into her pillow. Soon finding her pillow cold and wet with tears, she lifted her head and turned the pillow over. Paul's absence weighed heavy on her soul and her heart. What would she do? How could she get through the rest of this horrid war without seeing him? And what if he died?

Paul was right. Love did hurt. But love was also sacrifice. She would continue to love him, no matter what.

She heard giggling behind her. Ann and Julia were sharing a private joke.

Would she ever be able to laugh again?

***

Hannah ascended the stairs. Sister Betty had asked her to bring some files to the new surgeon. "New surgeon?" Hannah had asked. "What happened to Dr. K?"

Sister Betty sighed. "He's been transferred to the front."

"Oh, dear." Hannah couldn't help but be disappointed. After all, she hadn't yet had an opportunity to proposition Dr. Tall and Handsome again and now she'd never have another chance. *Well, at least Charlotte doesn't have him either.* That thought gave Hannah great comfort.

Chapter Eighteen
Dangerous Front

Paul spent the first two days of his new assignment acclimating himself to the less-than-adequate working conditions at the front. His quarters were composed of a small, crude tent and a more crude operating area.

And the noise. The shells sounded like they were landing right next to his tent.

The selection process to determine which soldiers were untreatable and therefore, must be left to die shocked him the most. Back at the field hospital, they'd been deluged by thousands of men on only a few occasions and could at least make those destined to die comfortable. As surgeon in charge at the front, Paul could operate on only those men who had a good chance of surviving. It was harsher than the selection process used at the field hospital and he despised it.

The last surgeon who had worked here was an American. He was killed in action.

The only other medical personnel here were one nurse and two medics who routinely travelled with the stretcher-bearers to retrieve wounded from the battlefield.

The nurse, Sister Aggie, was a middle-aged British spinster with excellent medical skills. She was the sole reason anyone had survived in the past week before Paul had arrived.

He ordered one of the medics, an Aussie chap by the name of Young, to assist him in cleaning and sewing up a deep, open laceration on a man who would bleed to death if they didn't work fast. The medic was a quick study and soon the young man could clean and stitch up as well as Paul.

That night the shelling ceased, and Paul took the opportunity to catch a nap. He dreamed of Charlotte. Of course, he would dream of her. As he was driving here via an autocar, he had had an entire twenty minutes to think about her. And he had to admit that, despite his best intentions, he was falling in love with her.

He hadn't wanted to tell Charlotte that they couldn't see each other again. But the transfer to the front would help to keep her at arm's length.

She probably hated him. If she did, that would bother him. But he couldn't think of that now. He had to focus on his duties.

***

Each day became slightly better for Charlotte. Like it or not, Paul had made no commitment to her. They hadn't even experienced a proper courtship. All they did was spend a few days under siege, then met at the stone chapel three times. Hardly what one would call a romance. But it was as real a romance as Charlotte had ever encountered.

The worst part about it was that she couldn't confide any of this information with her friend Julia. Some of the medical volunteers and sisters suspected there might've been something more than a friendship between her and Paul, but now? As much as she wished she did, she had nothing to share – not anymore.

***

The next day Paul woke to the sound of shelling. This time, it was undoubtedly closer than the battlefield. His ears were still ringing half an hour later. Unlike at the Vauxbuin Field Hospital, however, they would not receive orders to evacuate this close to the front. Then again, it was just Paul, two medics, three stretcher-bearers and one nursing sister. There was no choice. They had to remain. That was part of the danger of working at the front.

He dragged himself out of bed. The day before, he had saved four men who probably would have died without immediate treatment. Six other men had injuries that were too extensive, so they were kept as comfortable as possible, and all had died before the end of the day. He quickly washed and pulled on a clean pair of trousers.

Sister Aggie called to him. "Doctor, would you like a cup of coffee?"

"Yes, Sister, thank you."

Sister spent much of her spare time holding the men's hands and listening to their ramblings. Before one of the men had passed, Aggie had him chuckling at her sense of humour.

Leaning down, he pulled the blanket up to his pillow. Part of an envelope peeked out from under his pillow, and he took it out and read it again.

The more he denied his affection – even love – for Charlotte, the more it seemed to grow. This was the only correspondence he had received from her. It expressed anger that he didn't tell her in advance of his going to the front. He understood her anger – and even smiled because he was glad she felt that way. He could almost hear her words in a high-pitched yell. Yes, it was good that she was mad at him.

Then he read the rest of the letter where she had written, "I know love hurts, because it's hurting right now, but I'll love you no matter what, Paul."

He shoved her one and only letter under his pillow. The part of him that desired to be close to her desperately wanted to write to her. But his rational self didn't want to risk giving his heart to her because he knew from experience that the happiness of love and marriage couldn't be sustained. Too many things could go wrong and Paul would not risk it. Charlotte would just have to forget about him and get on with her life.

Chapter Nineteen
No Time for Brooding

Charlotte awoke each morning, recited her prayers, and focused on the soldiers in the death ward. Each day began with a new hope that perhaps she could do more for the soldiers in her care. Maybe if she prayed harder, sang better or gave them more comfort, they would have the will to live longer.

But every soldier moved to the death ward would die. The only variable was how soon after he arrived. And when a soldier died, she would write his name in her little notebook.

The death ward was quiet this afternoon. She had just finished reading to a semi-conscious soldier. He now slept peacefully, and she yawned. She startled when Sister Betty's voice boomed behind her.

"Charlotte, you've been working thirty-six hours straight. It's time to take a break. Go to the dorm and take a nap."

"Very well, Sister."

She exited the death ward, shuffled across the short lawn to the *chateau* and dragged her feet up the stairs to the dormitory. Charlotte was more tired than she dared to admit. But she preferred not to sleep unless brought about by exhaustion because when she slept, she dreamt of Paul.

And yet, as she lay on her cot, the mid-afternoon sun shone through the blinds, and even though she closed her eyes, her body refused to relax. Too many thoughts swirled around in her mind. *Is Paul safe?*

Charlotte was afraid for Paul because of his proximity to the front. And in the two weeks since he had been gone, she received no letters, despite the short letter she had sent him after he had left. Her words might have been curt, but they were nonetheless heartfelt, confirming her love for him, no matter how he treated her. She chose to love him unconditionally and completely. Not that he promised to write, of course. In fact, he was honest enough to say they should stop seeing each other. If he felt that way, he certainly wasn't planning to write. But it didn't matter. He was under a tremendous amount of stress as he struggled through the grief of losing his fiancée. She could only imagine how much anxiety he must be experiencing working at the front.

Charlotte promised herself that she would continue to pray for him, even if they weren't meant to be together.

She got up, went to the desk by the window, and took out a piece of paper. She jotted down a few lines telling Paul that she was praying for him every day. She ended it with, "I'll love you always." Slipping it into an envelope, she left it on the side of the desk to mail when she woke up.

Just last week, her dear friend Julia had also just been transferred to Le Tréport on the coast of France. Ann had gone there a few weeks ago. They were fortunate to be with Ella, the nurse who traveled with them to Europe. There were moments Charlotte felt lonely and wished she could go home stateside. But there would be no going home until this horrific war ended. And what would she go home to anyway? Everyone in her family was gone. A few neighbors back home and the dear pastor of her church were kind people, but they all had their own blood relatives. In many respects, she felt closer to the people at the field hospital.

She finally drifted off to sleep, a prayer for Paul's safety the last thought on her heart.

***

On a warm afternoon in late September, Charlotte figured she had at least an hour and a half before it would get dark and found herself strolling towards the back of the *chateau*. She kept her uniform and headscarf on, just in case there were incoming wounded.

Of course, she wasn't wandering aimlessly.

She followed the path along the edge of the forest. A warm breeze caressed her face, and she breathed in deeply the summer scents of the forest beside her. The sun behind her caused the trees to cast shadows next to her. She reached the chapel and placed her hand on the cool stone.

How she missed Paul.

This place seemed like so much more than a medieval stone shed. She wasn't sure whether it was the cross at the top of this building or her intuition. But this *had* to be a sacred place.

After praying for Paul and for her family in heaven, Charlotte caught sight of two caterpillars inching their way across the side of the structure. The sun was still making its presence known through the upper leaves of the trees. Charlotte followed the insects to the back end of the shed and into a – she gasped. There was a second entrance to this chapel, but this one was only partially blocked.

Using both hands, she worked a few heavy stones away from the opening and then stuck her head inside. It was dark, but she waited for her eyes to adjust. Sunlight beamed in through many small holes and two tiny windows.

She straightened, pulling back from the opening, and scanned her surroundings. Leaves swayed in a gentle breeze. Bugs chirped in nearby overgrown bushes. Her gaze turned back to the stone chapel. It beckoned to her.

Excitement and curiosity building inside her, she grabbed another stone and maneuvered it from the wall. Then she reached for a smaller one, then another rock until the opening was large enough to fit her body. ·

She crawled inside through the narrow entrance. As her eyes adjusted to the dimness, Charlotte glimpsed cobwebs and, arms flailing, swiped them away. A small spider fell on her hand. With a gasp, she flicked it away.

The inside was surprisingly comfortable and cool, and the cushion of moss below felt spongy under her shoes.

Charlotte was able to straighten, but her head was almost touching the roof. She stepped carefully, making sure she wouldn't crush any insects or small rodents that happened to be there. A high-pitched and almost inaudible squeak made her gasp. *A mouse?* She hoped she hadn't stepped on his tail.

Lumber sat against the far wall and something else, a long round – possibly metal – device against the opposite wall. A metal milk pail stood upright beside the wall she leaned against.

This ancient chapel seemed so far away from the war. She took a hand towel from her apron pocket and put it on the ground, then sat down and leaned her head against the stone wall. Whenever Charlotte felt the need to escape back home in the states, she always went to the church and sat in the quiet presence of Christ.

This wasn't a church, but it was a sacred place.

Her eyes felt heavy.

"Charli, when are you going to admit that I run faster than you?"

"Never. Because you don't."

"Oh, yeah? Watch me!"

Now that Ian was taller than she was, Charlotte couldn't outrun him. What a pest he was. Nine years old and already taller and stronger than she.

She roused as a rodent scurried over her lap. Gasping, she hoped it hadn't been a rat. As much as she had great affection for all animals, rats were the exception. She was once chased by one of those wretched rodents in the alleyway near her home back in Camden.

Judging by the light still streaming in through the tiny holes, it was still before sunset. She needed to leave before dark.

As she turned to leave, she glimpsed legs through the opening she had made at the back of the chapel. Someone walked by! She jerked back.

Before she could make sense of what she had seen, rock scraped against rock beside her. She tensed, her heart pounding. She followed the sound to the ground near the milk pail. A shaft of light lit up the pail and a large hairy hand thrust through the new hole.

Charlotte shuddered. The hand picked up what appeared to be a scroll and slipped back out of the hole. Whoever's hand that was, he had a tattoo on the inside of the wrist.

She exhaled, though her heart wouldn't calm, and she couldn't tear her gaze from the hole in the wall.

A moment passed before the hand returned to deposit another scroll. As she got a closer look, it was actually a rolled-up sheet of paper. As the man withdrew his hand,

Charlotte studied the inside of his wrist. There was a coiled snake tattoo.

Scraping and scratching noises, then it became darker as the man plugged the hole.

Charlotte held her breath. Would that man try to come inside?

When his footsteps became distant, she relaxed against the cool wall. From what she'd glimpsed of his olive drab uniform pants – and the puttee bound about his lower legs – she was pretty sure he was British.

What was *he* doing there?

She remained inside the stone chapel, waiting until she could no longer hear footsteps and was sure that he wouldn't come back. Rustling outside the chapel made her squeeze her eyes shut and shove herself against the wall. If that man was returning, he couldn't find her here.

Peering out the small window, she saw a deer running off into the forest. Charlotte sighed, relieved.

That man had just taken something from the side of the stone chapel. Charlotte turned toward the metal milk pail. It was now nearly dark. She wouldn't be able to read the rolled paper without light, but what in the world was going on? If only Paul were here. He would know what to do. To be safe, she decided not to touch it. Maybe it was nothing. Somehow, though, Charlotte was certain it was something important.

Chapter Twenty
Getting to the Bottom of It

Charlotte thought of the mystery of the man with the hairy hand and the tattoo. She had imagined all kinds of sordid scenarios but had no time to return to the stone chapel. By the weekend, her curiosity could not restrain itself, so she went back to the stone chapel to investigate. A cool mist hung in the air, but the daylight would allow her to clearly see whatever was behind the stone wall.

Approaching the area, Charlotte faced the side of the chapel. Should she go inside again and look at the paper or just do what the man did, retrieve it from the outside? She shook her head. Inside would be preferable. Then no one would see her studying it.

She squeezed inside the back entrance of the chapel, then went right to the milk pail. Crouching, she reached inside. Her fingers brushed against something. The paper, if it *was* the same paper, was still there. She brought the rolled-up note to the little window to read. Opening it, her heart raced. The words were German – so she couldn't understand them – and at the top of the paper – a drawing of a coiled snake.

What should she do about the note? There was only one thing she could do: return the note to the pail and report the incident to someone at the *chateau*. But who? Sister Betty was her supervisor, but would the woman know what to do or to whom they should give the information?

She started to stand, then she heard footsteps and muffled voices and a female giggling. Lifting her head and peering through the small window, Charlotte squinted. About fifty feet away, a medical aid worker with a headscarf leaned against the oak tree and the man – the British stretcher-bearer who had "propositioned" her a few weeks ago – had his hands on the girl's shoulder. She found out later that his name was Private Cal Harrison.

Charlotte backed away from the window. When she heard no more voices, she peeked and saw the couple kissing. Charlotte hoped Cal and the woman would leave so she could come out of her hiding place.

The girl spoke loudly, demonstrably. "Let's go back inside the *chateau*. It's dreadfully hot out here, and there are too many bugs."

It was the voice of Hannah Greene.

Moments later, Charlotte was finally able to emerge from the stone chapel. Part of her relished having the information that Hannah and Cal were "fraternizing." Of course, the more virtuous part of her – and her conscience – told her that she should not share that information with anyone. She *must* turn the other cheek, no matter how Hannah had treated her. Besides, she had more important matters to deal with. She must inform someone in charge about the paper hidden in the stone chapel, the paper with German words on it.

Chapter Twenty-One
A Critically Wounded Soldier

The Huns were getting tired and desperate. But in their desperation, they became more brutal. Half of the men that came to Paul were too far-gone, and all he could do was to try to keep them comfortable with morphine in their last hours. He listened to more than a few men plead, *Please tell my wife, my girlfriend, my beloved I love her.* If he kept track of every dying soldier who had said similar words in the past week, Paul wouldn't have had time to operate on the men who needed him.

If only he could save more men. That was the reason he was at the front. In actuality, many of the injuries were beyond what modern medicine could remedy. The most recent wounds were becoming more brutal compared to when he started working here at the front. He chalked it up to the extreme savagery caused by desperation.

The war would soon end, but not soon enough for Paul.

Earlier in the morning, Paul had time to take a quick shower before another group of men were brought to him. The first man had a gaping hole in his midsection and a weak pulse. He gave him a shot of morphine. There was nothing more he could do for that man. Another soldier had superficial leg wounds that could wait until he got to a field hospital. The stretcher-bearers took the two men in an ambulance and sped off.

A soldier ran toward the tent, his hand across his stomach, the dark crimson fluid spurting from his midsection. From the man's uniform, Paul knew he was an American.

"Over here!" Paul rushed out to assist the man to the tent and shouted for Aggie. Once inside, Paul lifted the soldier onto a table. This man was losing blood rapidly, but Paul's specialty was abdominal wounds, so he was certain he could save him.

"Aggie, give him a shot of morphine." He then instructed the nurse to administer a mixture of chloroform and ether to put him to sleep. With no other casualties at present, Paul took his time cleaning the wound, which had exposed part of his lower intestines and had nicked the abdominal aorta. He repaired the aorta, but the intestines would take longer.

"Need any help there, sir?" said a medic who stood behind him.

The interruption broke Paul's concentration. "Uh, no, we're fine."

An hour later, Paul completed the job and called to the stretcher-bearers. "This one is ready to be transported." As he called, the patient roused, the ether/chloroform gas wearing off.

"Am...am I going to...die?"

"No, sir, you are not going to die. We're just sending you to the field hospital."

"May I know the name of the man who has saved my life?"

"Dr. Paul Kilgallen. Just doing my duty, Corporal."

"Thank you, sir. My wife and unborn child thank you, as well as my —"

"Shhh. No need, soldier. No need."

As the ambulance truck drove off, Aggie quipped, "That man probably has no idea how close he came to death."

"Hopefully he'll recover and return home to see his wife and baby."

Chapter Twenty-Two
The Return of a Friend

Charlotte burst through the doors of the *chateau*, anxious to share the information about the stone chapel and the paper. The time was now five minutes to two in the afternoon. Sister Betty usually had tea in the dining hall every afternoon around two unless there were incoming wounded.

In the dining hall, she found Sister Betty sipping her tea and eating what looked like a stale biscuit. After she told her story, Sister waved her hand dismissively and chuckled. "That note could've been left there years ago, even before the war."

"But I saw someone place the paper in there."

"You saw them?"

"Yes. I was inside the stone chapel."

"The what?"

"The stone chapel. There's an old stone structure on the edge of the forest behind the *chateau*."

"There is? Very well. When the commander of the unit visits tomorrow, I will inform him, and he can decide what to do about it."

"Thank you, Sister."

"My pleasure."

***

Charlotte tried not to think too much about the paper or the man with the hairy hand and the tattoo. Part of her was annoyed. She had used that ancient chapel to pray and reflect – and to think of Paul. Now, she felt as if someone had trespassed on her special place.

When her friend, Julia, returned to the field hospital from Le Treport, Charlotte hoped that it would mend her broken heart and distract her from thoughts of espionage. And Julia's visit did help her, to a certain extent. Julia shared with Charlotte how she found Major Winslow in Le Treport and had finally realized that *he* was, in fact, her beloved. Major Winslow had even asked her to marry him. It was right out of a fairy tale, whereas Charlotte's story seemed more like a tragedy.

Poor Julia was truly missing her fiancé, and Charlotte wished that she could share her own feelings about Paul. However, there wasn't really anything to share. She couldn't say, "I've been praying for Dr. K every day because I love him, even though he doesn't love me," because it was *not* something Charlotte wanted to share.

Envy reached its ugly head to the surface. Charlotte was happy for her friend, so she pushed back the envy. Julia was blessed to have a man who returned her love, and Charlotte was happy for her friend.

***

Hannah despised this war. She despised not being able to take a warm shower every day. She despised not having enough food. She despised the backbreaking work. It was already October, but it was still dreadfully hot. She longed for a cool, steamed tea with lots of lemon. She sighed. Cal had made the time pass a bit more quickly, but even *he* became boring. He wanted to see her all the time, especially now that she had given him what he wanted. Men, they were all the same.

Chapter Twenty-Three
Lesson from a Dying Man

October 24, 1918

Today Paul was able to save three more men. A young Brit was too far-gone, and there was nothing else Paul could do for him. Aggie had accompanied the ambulance to the hospital in Soissons, and the two medics had gone into the battlefield to treat men there. It was left to Paul to console this young man.

The poor soldier had a large piece of shrapnel through his chest just below his heart. If Paul tried to remove the shrapnel, the man would die within seconds. The piece of metal was actually prolonging his life. The young man was bleeding slowly enough that he had minutes, maybe half an hour, till death, but death would surely come.

The soldier, he discovered, despite his terminal injuries, was not only chatty, but also rational. In fact, he spoke in a rapid-fire manner as if there were nothing wrong with him. When the man did pass, it would be quick, so Paul continued listening to him. That made it all the more difficult waiting for him to die.

"'ave ye got a wife, Doc?" the man said in a cockney accent.

"No, no, I haven't." Thoughts of Charlotte came to his mind. Strange, though, since he was only ever close to marrying one girl, Catherine. Why didn't *she* come to his mind?

"Just got married before I 'nlisted. Jus' turned nineteen an' me wife's 'bout ready to pop. I told 'er it's a boy, but she thinks it's a girl."

Paul cringed and squeezed the man's hand. This young father-to-be would never live to see his child, regardless of its gender.

"Me wife, her name's Lynn, she dinna wanna get married in case something 'appened to me, ye know? And I told 'er, I said, Lynn, darlin', even if somethin' 'appens to me, we still 'ave our love. And now that love is a little baby that's gonna carry my name."

Despite his condition, the man grinned from ear to ear. "And you know what, Doc? That love 'as gotten me through the past seven months at the front. Thinkin' of Lynn and our babe and how good God's been te us. Just can't believe I'm gonna be a father. Last year I was going te school and not even kissed a girl. This year, Lynn and me, we got married, and I'm gonna be a father."

Paul nodded and held onto the man's hand. Judging by the amount of blood dripping onto the floor below him, Paul figured that this poor fellow only had a few minutes more to live.

"Doc?"

"Hmm?" Paul leaned close to the man's face.

"In case I don't make it, will ye make sure me wife knows I love 'er and our babe? Me name's Private Ernie Powell. Wife's name is Lynn. Address is 272 Winifred Lane, Liverpool..."

Just then, the man stopped talking and his hand fell limp. He stopped breathing. Though his eyes remained open, he could no longer see.

Hearing the *camion* return, Paul called out to Aggie.

"Yes, Doctor?"

"Would you please write down this information for me?"

Aggie glanced down at the man on the table. "Of course." She reached into her front apron pocket and pulled out a pencil and small scrap of paper. "Go ahead."

"Mrs. Ernie Powell, 272 Winifred Lane, Liverpool. Please jot down that her husband died... and wanted to tell her...that he loves her...and their baby." He couldn't believe he was getting choked up. He cleared his voice. "Thank you. Please get that in the post as soon as you can."

"Yes, Doctor."

Now alone in the small operating tent, Paul closed the man's eyes and placed a sheet over his head. He would be placed on the ambulance for the next trip into Soissons.

Back in his private tent, Paul sat on his bunk, head in his hands. "Eternal rest grant unto him, oh Lord, and let perpetual light shine upon him. May Private Powell's soul rest in peace. Amen."

He sat up straight and cocked his head. He hadn't prayed in two years – well, that wasn't true. He prayed that God would bring back Catherine, but he realized that that had been an unreasonable request. Even as he thought of his fiancée, he could not get Charlotte out of his mind. And the more he thought of her, the less he thought of his fiancée. In fact, he couldn't even conjure up Catherine's face in his mind and immediately felt guilty.

Paul and his fiancée had been only days away from marrying. How could he stop thinking of her? How could he *not* stop thinking about Charlotte? He tilted his head and nearly laughed out loud. He couldn't stop thinking about Charlotte because he was alive.

Well, he was alive, but he hadn't truly been living. Pushing people away, avoiding his family, ignoring God, joining this wretched war. Yes, he was saving other people's lives, but why had he made such a mess of his own?

Yes, love hurt, but love also brought joy.

Charlotte had looked so hurt when he told her they should stop seeing each other and that he was being transferred to the front. He had known Private Powell for less than an hour, and yet that man taught him more about living than anyone had ever taught him. Live life to the fullest, no matter how much time one has left.

Chapter Twenty-Four
I Once Was Lost

The end of October brought cooler temperatures and memories of bobbing for apples and carving jack-o'-lanterns with her brother. Charlotte would give anything to have him back. Sighing, she focused on the task in front of her: washing bandages by hand and hanging them to dry. It hardly seemed like an important job, but alas, it was. The war would come to an end soon, but clean bandages were still needed for war wounds.

The decrease in the number of battles, the western front now back to the original place near the Belgium border and fewer critically wounded soldiers meant there was no longer a need for the separate death ward. A few soldiers were still deemed terminal, but Charlotte had become so well-known at the field hospital as a singing angel for dying men that whenever a man was close to death, someone would find her, and she would hold hands, hum a quiet song, and whisper calming words to him until he passed. She still held out hope each time that each soldier might live, but that never seemed to happen.

Charlotte now spent most days in preparation for the war's end, which was estimated to be as soon as the Axis countries signed the offer from the Allies.

There were wounded men left, however, and Charlotte was always relieved when she could interact and assist those soldiers.

She'd heard no news regarding the note left by the man with the tattoo in the stone chapel. Did Sister Betty even tell the person in charge about it?

As she was hanging the last bit of washed bandages over the line, she heard the high-pitched laughter of a young man. She straightened and shook her head. *That man's laugh sounds exactly like Ian's.* Her brother had the oddest of cackles, but apparently it wasn't that odd. *Did someone steal Ian's laugh?*

Whenever she thought of Ian, she offered up a prayer for his soul. "Please take care of him in heaven, Blessed Mother." Wiping her moist eyes, basket in hand, she turned.

The source of the laughter was a soldier and – it looked like – his very pregnant wife. The soldier was dressed in fatigues, but the woman wore a beautiful pink-patterned dress. *Aren't they blessed?*

As she stared blankly at the couple, she heard the name that only her brother and father had called her. "Charli! Charli!!" She blinked, then she shifted her gaze to the young soldier's face. *Dear Lord, how can it be? He was dead, wasn't he? No, this is a dream. This must be a dream.*

The man rushed toward Charlotte with ferocity, and he gave her a tight embrace.

She stepped back. Was this really happening? Was her brother alive? She stared, mouth open, but couldn't bring herself to say his name.

"Charli! It's me! I can't believe you're over here. I haven't heard from you in over a year!"

Finally, she stammered. "I...I... thought...you...."

"What?"

"I thought you were...I got a telegram saying you...were...dead." Charlotte could barely get the words out.

Ian's smile faded. "I was captured by the Huns, spent seven months in a prisoner camp and was lucky enough to escape. My tags were pulled off in a struggle and left in the battlefield. Perhaps that's why they thought I had died. After a leave in Paris, I've been on the battlefields since March."

"I've been *here* since March."

"Charli, I can't tell you how –"

Charlotte hugged him again to prove to herself he was really there. Ian protested, "Not too tightly, sis. I had a pretty serious wound in my stomach. But I'm going to be okay. I thought I was a goner."

As they laughed, Charlotte noticed the young pregnant woman standing behind them, a wide smile on her face.

Ian turned and took the girl's hand. "Charli, I'd like to introduce you to my wife, Zélie Marie Zielinski, about to give birth to our baby in a month or so, as you can see."

Charlotte could only nod. Not only had her brother come back from the dead, but he was also married to a beautiful girl with a child on the way.

Zélie held her hand out. "I am so very pleased to meet Ian's sister. You are exactly as Ian has described." Ian's wife spoke English with only a bit of an accent.

Charlotte shook the girl's hand at first tentatively, then more enthusiastically. "I am so pleased to meet you."

Ian brought both women into an embrace. "I can't believe it! I'm with my two favorite girls in the whole world!"

Charlotte was still in a daze. Ian was alive and on the mend. Married and a father. And Charlotte would be an aunt. There was just too much information to take in at once. She reveled in the embrace of her family, a family that was once lost and was now found. She never wanted to let them go.

Chapter Twenty-Five
Near Miss

It was Friday morning, November 1, All Saints Day. Paul might not have been practicing his faith over here, but he hadn't forgotten the holy days of obligation. Yesterday was Halloween, and he spent it restfully with no wounded and no surgical procedures. He hoped today would be the same.

Paul wondered whether the children in the neighbouring town had gone from house to house dressed in costumes. Probably not. Traditions were different here in Europe.

It was a quiet morning, too quiet, in fact. He sat outside his tent and gazed upward. Even the birds were silent. Paul preferred the sounds of the fighting to the silence. When the enemy attacked with bombs and artillery, he knew where they were.

The ambulance drove up, and Aggie and the medic got out.

He rose from the chair outside his tent and greeted them. Aggie held her hand out, an envelope in her palm. "You have a letter, Paul."

"Thank you, Aggie."

Paul turned the letter over. *From Charlotte*. He closed his eyes and sighed.

He returned to his tent and placed the envelope on his desk beside his cot. He wasn't ready to read her letter...not yet.

After consuming three cups of weak coffee this morning, Paul had to relieve himself, so he walked about fifty feet beyond his tent.

***

Despite the happiness at having her brother "return from the dead," Charlotte's feelings were a mixture of overwhelming joy and melancholy. She kept pinching herself to ensure that she wasn't dreaming that Ian was alive.

It was the Feast of All Saints. Charlotte wished she could attend Mass. Instead, she visited the stone chapel. She kept forgetting to ask Sister Betty whether anything was done about the German note. Until she heard otherwise, the stone chapel was safe.

She prayed that her Guardian Angel would attend Mass for her and prayed for her beloved parents. As her thoughts turned to Paul, a sense of urgency struck her, compelling her to pray for him. "Jesus, Mary, and Joseph, watch over Paul. Keep him safe."

***

Paul had just finished relieving himself when an explosion went off behind him, propelling him several feet into the brush. He landed facedown on the dirt, his ears ringing. Pushing himself up, his back stung as if pierced by a hot metal poker.

His ears were still ringing when he finally turned around.

Stumbling ahead, dirt and dust filled the air, so he had to hold his shirtsleeve up to his mouth. His comrades would need help. He had to get to them.

He tripped, then steadied himself to remain standing. Something lay in his path, at his feet...an odd branch? No, something blood-red covered half of it. Wait. Was it....

A wave of nausea hit him, and he gasped. It was the leg of the medic.

Good God. Where's Aggie?

As the air cleared, Paul coughed up more dirt and scanned his surroundings. The extent of the devastation soon revealed itself, and he found himself staggering back.

There was no medical tent, no sleeping tents, just bits and pieces of canvas, tables, chairs, and equipment. His eyes focused on a partial body that used to be Aggie's, clothed in white, with surprisingly little blood, and just beyond her, a good portion of the medic's body. No need to determine whether they were alive since their still bodies and conditions were incongruent with life. *Rest in peace.*

He searched for linen to cover them, but there were only shreds of cloth.

The ambulance lay on its side twenty feet away, but still intact. Footsteps ahead of him made him stumble to the ambulance to take cover behind it. His body trembled, and everything moved slowly. Paul shivered, and his teeth chattered. He recognized the symptoms of shock, but there was little he could do, other than wait and see who approached.

Voices nearby spoke, but he couldn't decipher what they said or even what language they spoke. Was it English? Was it German? French? Why couldn't he – in that moment between consciousness and unconsciousness, Paul had one regret: that he had not told Charlotte he loved her.

***

Charlotte couldn't stop thinking about Paul. Was he all right? At the front, anything could happen. And whether he was in danger or not, praying for someone was always a good thing. *Please, God, keep Paul safe and let this awful war end soon.*

***

Paul roused as he slid across the floor of a vehicle – an ambulance? He hoped so. He tried to open his eyes, but his lids were too heavy. He'd obviously lost more blood than he originally thought. If he could barely open his eyes, it meant he was close to exsanguination. *Please, God, help me. I want to live.*

Chapter Twenty-Six
An Unusual Honor

The first Sunday of November brought a fine mist of rain and a cloudy day. It was the first time that she, Ian, and Zélie could attend Mass together as a family. When one of the Army chaplains visited the field hospital a few days ago, she told him about the stone chapel behind the *chateau*. He agreed to hold Mass at this most beautiful – and sacred – place. Since it wasn't large enough to hold more than six or seven people, chairs had been set up outside, facing the front of the structure.

Her friend Julia sat with them. It was a solemn low Mass, and Charlotte could feel the hopefulness of all those attending that soon the war would finally and officially cease.

After Mass, the small group walked to the dining area for a light lunch. Ian was scheduled to be released soon, and he would be returning to the States with his new wife. He then planned to search for a job that would enable him to support his wife and soon-to-be-born child.

The girl that Ian had chosen to marry was not only pretty on the outside, she was also sweet-natured on the inside. Zélie had told Charlotte that she and Ian had met during his leave in Paris, after Ian had spent seven months in a prisoner-of-war camp. She told Charlotte that Ian had been thin but still had a spark in his eyes and a constant smile on his face. Charlotte could imagine her brother, despite his capture and whatever ill treatment he had endured, being positive and never losing hope. Charlotte tried very much to emulate Ian in that regard.

Listening to Zélie speak of their love and romance made Charlotte envious again. She forced the envy away, and in its place, embraced joy and happiness for her brother and his new wife.

Charlotte still thought of Paul when she woke up, and he was the last thing on her mind when she went to sleep. She stopped trying to erase him from her mind. Instead, every time she thought of him, she offered a prayer for him.

"Charlotte!" Sister Betty called from the door of the dining room. "You have what looks to be an important letter from the post."

Ripping it open, Charlotte read that she and Paul had been recommended for one of France's highest honors, the Legion of Honor "for bravery and fortitude during battle." Farther down in the letter, it said, "There will be an inquiry to determine and confirm that both parties do not have a criminal record and that both parties are of good character."

Sister Betty, who was leaning over her shoulder as she read, spoke up. "It's highly unusual to give this to anyone for a one-time event."

"Really?"

"But it's well-deserved, Charlotte."

"Thank you, Sister." She paused. "Does this mean that Dr. Kilgallen will have to attend the inquiry or the award ceremony?"

"No to both. I suspect that the inquiry is a formality to ensure that you're both of good character, and the award can always be sent by post to the recipient. The recipients are only called to attend if there are reports of poor character."

Staring down, Charlotte scanned the letter for the date of inquiry and read it out loud. "November 12th." She looked up. "That's only nine days away."

"I wouldn't worry, my dear. Your good character is well-known." Sr. Betty left.

Hearing footsteps behind her, Charlotte turned. Ian's happy face greeted her. "Hello, Charli. I'm not certain from your expression whether you are happy or just concerned about something."

"Happy. I just received this letter saying that Dr. K and I will be receiving the Legion of Honor for courage."

"That's outstanding, sis! Who's Dr. K?"

"Yes, his name is Paul."

When she glanced at Ian, he was scowling. "What's going on with this Paul fellow?"

"What do you mean?"

"Come on, Charli. I've known you your whole life. You just said his name as if it were a piece of fine chocolate."

"I love him, but he doesn't love me. End of story."

"I can't believe he doesn't love you."

"Well, believe it. Dr. Paul Kilgallen does not love me but will be receiving an award with me."

Ian's face blanched. "Dr. Paul...Kilgallen is the other person who will be receiving this award...." he stuttered to finish. "And the man you love?"

"Yes, what's wrong?"

"He's the doctor who saved my life."

Charlotte's mouth hung open, but she couldn't find her voice.

"He saved my life, Charli." He pointed to his abdomen. "I would've been dead without his handiwork. The doctor here told me I was very lucky that Dr. K. was at the front. Without him, I would never have made it to the field hospital."

Charlotte's eyes clouded with unshed tears.

Ian pulled her into an embrace. "Your beau saved my life. If that isn't fate, I don't know what is."

"He's...not my beau, Ian. He doesn't love me."

Ian held her at arm's length. "But you love him. I can tell, Charli. The way you talk about this man, you love him."

She straightened. "Yes."

"Well, then he's an idiot. I don't care if he saved my life. Anyone who doesn't love you is a fool."

Nodding, she hugged her brother again, this time, taking advantage of his shirtsleeve to wipe her eyes.

"Hey, I've got a handkerchief for that, sis." He took out his handkerchief and handed it to her.

Wiping her eyes, she couldn't believe that Paul had saved her brother. She may never have his love, but she would always be grateful to him for saving Ian.

***

Standing at the window in the far end of the second-floor hallway, Hannah peered down as Charlotte walked across the short lawn to the death ward. Hannah's breathing became rapid, and she lifted her chin. So Charlotte and Dr. K would be receiving an award? There was just no end to that girl always getting what she wanted.

She scoffed, thankful that recent casualties were light, and she now had respite from the backbreaking work.

Footfalls behind her made her roll her eyes. She knew it was Cal from the way he snuck up on her. Before he touched her, she turned and said, "Hello, Cal."

"Hey, doll. Want to go find a quiet place and –"

"No."

"Come on. The war's almost over. I can feel it." He pulled her into an embrace, and she pushed him away.

"Not in the mood, Cal."

"What's wrong, baby?"

"Charlotte and Dr. K will be receiving an award for their supposed courage because they stayed behind during the battle in July."

"And?"

"Some girls have all the luck."

"She thinks she's better than us anyway."

Hannah scoffed.

Cal winked. "Now, where were we?" He leaned in to kiss her.

***

Charlotte had worked in Barrack 29 for most of the week. Her duties included changing dressings and giving hypodermics. While thankful that fewer men were near death, she missed being able to form a bond with the soldiers. But at least these men didn't die.

"Charlotte?" The voice came from behind. She turned to see Sister Betty approaching.

Wringing her hands, the woman hesitated before speaking. "I thought you should know."

"Know what?"

The woman glanced away. "Dr. Kilgallen was injured at the medic station near the front."

Charlotte's heart skipped a beat, and her ears started to ring. Finally, she responded, "Injured?"

"Yes, but an acquaintance of mine at the hospital in Soissons says he's recuperating there."

Taking a deep breath and releasing it slowly, Charlotte finally asked, "He's going to be all right?"

"Yes. Although I hear he's been a bit of a difficult patient."

Charlotte smiled inwardly. She could imagine that.

"We expect him to come to the field hospital for the award."

Later that night, as she lay in bed, Charlotte reflected on her gratitude to Paul. To have her beloved brother back in her life was an answer to a prayer that she had never thought to pray.

Paul had been injured but was now recuperating. She couldn't stop her heart from racing at the thought of seeing him again. Placing her palm in the middle of her chest, she forced her heart to slow down. Paul wasn't interested in her that way; he didn't want to commit. He was still grieving, and she would respect that. Of all people, she knew what it was like to grieve.

Charlotte wished she could visit him at the hospital in

Soissons to thank him for saving her brother's life and—
No, that wouldn't be wise. She must wait until he arrived
for the award ceremony.

When she did finally see him, she would be as kind and
unemotional as she could, although the extent of her
gratitude for saving Ian's life might be too strong for her to
restrain. She would give him the firmest – and most
sisterly – hug that she could muster.

With Ian back in her life, she now had family, a new
sister and a new niece or nephew coming. Charlotte would
continue her life, and she would continue loving Paul.

Chapter Twenty-Seven
Recuperation

Paul spent the first few days of November in surgery, then in and out of consciousness. But now, a week later, he despised being forced to rest when his injury was so minor. During the explosion, two pieces of shrapnel punctured his back, but the doctors had already removed them. His left kidney was nicked by shrapnel, but the other piece of shrapnel made superficial wounds, with no injuries to any other organs. In that regard, he was very, very lucky. He had, however, lost a fair amount of blood, but he was now feeling well enough to do anything but lie in bed.

The nurses and doctors here didn't seem to have much tolerance for him, though. They indicated to him that he was not a very good patient. Paul wasn't accustomed to being on the receiving end of care, and he hated it.

Besides, all this "resting" made him think continuously of Charlotte. Here at the hospital in Soissons, it was walking distance to the field hospital at Vauxbuin – a long walk of about five kilometers, but still a walk. It made it that much more frustrating that he was close, but he couldn't visit her. Maybe he should send her a letter? He could give it to one of the doctors and medics who visited the field hospital frequently. He shook his head. He needed to see her in person, face to face.

Once he was well enough to travel, the first thing he would do was visit the field hospital and tell Charlotte – no, not tell her, but ask her to marry him at the first available moment.

"Doctor Kilgallen?"

He looked up to see a young female medical volunteer dressed in blue and white holding something out to him. "You have a letter, sir."

"Thank you." Paul took it, his pulse quickened thinking it might be another letter from Charlotte. Instead, the back of it showed the address of the Government of France. He lifted his brows. *Why would the Government of France be contacting me?* He glanced at the postdate of two weeks ago. They had probably tried to deliver it to the medical unit at the front. But, of course, there was no longer a medical unit at the front. He lowered his head and said a prayer for his two comrades.

He ripped open the envelope and read quickly. He and Charlotte had been recommended for one of France's highest honors, the Legion of Honor "for bravery and fortitude during battle." He put the letter down. "The Legion of Honor? For bravery during the siege of Soissons?" He scoffed at the prospect of receiving a medal for doing his job.

He searched the letter for the date of the hearing and noted that it was tomorrow. While he had no obligation to attend, the idea of presenting himself at the hearing – and getting out of this hospital – tempted him.

Given the short notice, Paul decided to wait until he was well enough and visit the field hospital a few days before the ceremony.

Fiddle music – played passably – came from another

room on this floor of the hospital. He decided to get up and see where it was coming from. Pulling on his robe, Paul ventured into the hallway and followed the sound of the music. It wasn't his favorite sort of violin music, but at least the person played on key. Thoughts of Charlotte came to him. She couldn't play passably to save her life, but he found so many other things to love about her.

The music was louder now, and he peeked into one of the wardrooms to see an American soldier playing for the wounded men. Paul leaned against the wall and tapped his foot to the lively music.

***

Charlotte was thankful that the United States Army had given Ian permission to remain at the field hospital until the medal ceremony. Then he would be relieved of duty and return to the United States with his new bride. Until then, Zélie returned to visit her family in Paris. Ian busied himself with light duties such as assisting in the dining hall or peeling potatoes in the kitchen. In the weeks since he had been wounded, Ian had gone from critically injured to miraculously recovered, thanks, of course, to Paul's skill.

How was Paul doing at the hospital in Soissons? Charlotte prayed that he would recuperate quickly.

***

The upbeat music continued to play with a few men clapping along. Paul's attention was drawn to the back of the instrument and his eyes widened. There was no doubt. He'd seen that violin before.

Chapter Twenty-Eight
Surprise Find

When the man ceased playing, Paul approached him. "Sergeant?"

The soldier turned around. "Good day, sir. You're the doctor in the officers' ward, correct?"

"Yes, I am."

The man rolled his eyes, then forced a smile. Paul could only surmise that the staff's difficulties with him were known to the other patients.

"May I ask where you got that violin?" Paul asked.

"At the pawn shop in town. It was a real bargain."

"May I see it?"

"Of course."

Paul took it and examined it, noting especially the acorns and pinecones around the outside and the tree branches and cherubs in the centre. There was only one violin like this in the world. He checked it for Charlotte's father's initials. There they were in the bottom corner, "K.Z." *This is Charlotte's violin!*

"Sergeant, what did you pay for it?"

"It doesn't matter. I'm not letting this beauty out of my sight."

Paul sighed. "That's a stolen violin, Sergeant."

The man's face became white. "I...didn't... know."

"It was stolen from my..." Paul had no idea how he should refer to Charlotte. "...friend a few months ago."

"I see."

"It means a great deal to my friend because her father carved it for her."

The man's shoulders slumped. "I only paid twenty-five francs for it, which was a tremendous bargain."

"Indeed, it was. Priceless, really, when you consider the work her father put into it. His initials are in the bottom right-hand corner there." He pointed.

The man squinted, then nodded.

"Look, I'm willing to pay you quadruple what you paid, then I can give it back to my friend."

The man's head bowed, and he blew out a breath. "Very well."

Paul reached to shake the sergeant's hand. "I will have your money before I leave the hospital."

"All right."

***

The date for the hearing had arrived. Charlotte decided to visit the stone chapel on the edge of the forest before attending the hearing early that afternoon. She had worked late last evening, holding another soldier's hand as he entered eternity. After returning to the dorm, she tossed and turned for over an hour before falling asleep. Then she was awoken early by commotion in the hallway near the dormitory.

A thick mist clung to the area behind the *chateau*. As Charlotte walked, she breathed in deeply, reveling in the crisp scent of dry leaves and fresh autumn air. Maples, oaks and birch trees blazed with color against the gray fog. She pulled the shawl closer to her chest.

In the two or three times that she had come to the stone chapel, she had not seen or heard anyone else nearby, except when the chaplain held Mass here. Approaching the chapel, she squinted to make out the building in the thick fog. She was nearly on top of it before she realized it was right in front of her. Looking forward to the solitude, she lifted away a few large stones at the back entrance and crawled inside. This was a place where she could fully relax with no one to interrupt her thoughts and prayers. As usual, her first prayer was one of gratitude that her brother was alive and that he had a wife and child on the way. Her second prayer was for Paul. She was also thankful that whatever injuries he had endured at the front were no longer life-threatening.

God, I know You can do anything. I don't want to ask You to make Paul love me. If he isn't meant to be my husband.... She stopped. She had spent long hours with her beloved brother and was so joyful and thankful he was not dead. Yet, even with concentrating on the soldiers and in her brother's company for much of the time, she just couldn't seem to stop thinking about Paul.

Leaning her back against the stone, she gasped. The stone was as cold as an igloo. She wrapped her shawl tightly around her, then relaxed against the stone wall. *Lord, please make me forget Paul.*

It was her last thought before drifting off to sleep.

Charlotte's eyes flew open at a deafening crack nearby. Bits of wood and dirt from the stone chapel's roof spewed down on her. Her entire body shook from the impact. Other than that, the stone chapel seemed to have provided sanctuary from the explosion.

She crawled to the opening, then squeezed through the narrow hole and stood up. The fog hadn't yet dissipated, but smoke was now bellowing forth from the forest.

Curious, she inched toward the smoke. Still about twenty feet away, she came upon a huge crater with several trees splayed outward from the center. Paul had told her that the forest was to be avoided at all costs because of the possibility of previous battles' undetonated shells, but this was the first time she had ever encountered one. She knew better than to approach the area, and given the fact that nobody had arrived at the scene, she suspected this was an all-too-common occurrence. She recalled a few similar explosions that seemed to be closer than the front but had ignored them.

Just then, she peered down at her small watch on the front of her apron and drew in a breath. She must've fallen asleep for hours! The hearing would begin in a minute or two.

Charlotte turned and sprinted through the fog, trying to skip over the rocks that were strewn across the ground. As she passed by the oak tree, she knew the ruins of the old house were close and to the left. She stumbled over another group of rocks and hesitated to gain her footing.

She stepped onto what appeared to be a wooden plank, but the board disappeared below her, and she fell downward, her headscarf torn from her head.

Chapter Twenty-Nine
Missing Witness

Ian arrived at the dining hall well before the hearing but was astonished to find that Charli was nowhere to be seen. He tried not to worry. His sister often lost track of time. She'd be kicking herself about it afterwards, though.

The dining room had been set up as a temporary meeting place for the hearing. Ian sat in front, and he saved one of the chairs for her.

A man by the name of Monsieur Pierre Lalonde conducted the hearing. He was a tall, middle-aged chap with a bushy moustache.

Monsieur began by asking for witnesses to come forward to testify to both Charlotte's and Paul's character. Although the man was French, he spoke excellent English with a minimal accent.

Before the hearing began, Ian held his hand high.

"Yes, sir?"

"My sister is Miss Charlotte Zielinski, one of the subjects of this hearing. She is supposed to be here, but she's not. Is it possible to delay this at all?"

"It isn't necessary for Miss Zielinski to be present, Corporal Zielinski. We're just going to move forward with the inquiry."

Ian sighed, and his shoulders slumped. He supposed the man was correct, but now he was beginning to worry about Charli.

First, two of the British nursing sisters testified regarding Paul's character as well as Charlotte's. Then Ian and three medical aid volunteers came forward, along with a soldier who was terminally ill. Ian wasn't at all surprised at how highly Charli was regarded by her co-workers and others. To hear them speak, it sounded like Charli was on the road to sainthood. Then again, maybe that wasn't far off the mark.

Monsieur Lalonde thanked everyone and appeared to be closing the hearing. A man from the back of the room said, "I wish to testify about Miss Zielinski's character."

Not recognizing the voice or the accent, Ian turned. Something about him looked familiar, but he couldn't remember where he'd seen him before.

"Come forward," Monsieur Lalonde said. "What is your name, please?"

"Private Calvin Harrison, British Expeditionary Forces, stretcher-bearer."

"Private Harrison, do you wish to say something about Miss Zielinski's character?"

"Yes, I do," he said, his Cockney accent seeming more pronounced. Monsieur Lalonde swore Private Harrison in, then the man began to chat excitedly. "I know Charlotte quite well. In fact, we've been engaged in – let me put it this way – I *know* this young lady in the biblical sense, if ye get my meaning."

There was a collective and loud gasp from the rest of the attendees.

Ian's eyes widened, and he labored to breathe.

Why would this fellow lie?

Private Harrison continued. "And if ye consider that Miss Zielinski was alone with the doctor for three days straight, well, it's just scandalous."

Monsieur Lalonde said, "Thank you, sir." He motioned Private Harrison to take a seat.

"In light of the testimony of Private Harrison, and since most of the men who were in the basement with Miss Zielinski and Dr. Kilgallen are either deceased or have been relieved of duty, I think it would be prudent to bring Dr. Paul Kilgallen here to give testimony. And Miss Zielinski, if you are able to find her."

Sister Betty stood. "Sir, might I speak?"

"Yes, Sister."

"Dr. Kilgallen is presently at St. Paul's Hospital in Soissons. I'm sure that we can send someone to get him to testify, assuming he is well enough to travel."

"Yes, as long as he is fit enough to testify, by all means."

Ian turned to Sister Betty. "I'll get him, but someone needs to find Charlotte."

He strode to the front of the courtroom. "Sir, I'd be happy to fetch Dr. Kilgallen and bring him back straightaway."

"Thank you. This hearing is adjourned for one hour."

***

Darkness shadowed the hospital room. Although it was early afternoon, the day was foggy and rainy. Paul dressed and was preparing to inform his doctor that he was no longer staying in his cot. In fact, he was planning to check himself out later in the day, lest the boredom kill him before the injury. Besides, the wound was nearly healed and showed no sign of infection. He was ready to either start working at this hospital or head back to the field hospital. Of course, he had ulterior motives for going to the field hospital.

He stared out the window. The people of Soissons were starting to rebuild, but what a mess this town was with just about every building sustaining damage. Even the hospital needed major repairs.

"Dr. Kilgallen? Dr. Paul Kilgallen?"

He turned to find a young Yank with dark hair. The young man smiled and held out his hand, which Paul shook. Paul had met the man before but couldn't remember where.

"Yes..."

"My name is Corporal Ian Zielinski. You saved my life at the medic station at the front nearby."

"Ah, yes."

"Thank you, sir."

"No need. Just –"

"My sister needs your help."

"Your sister?"

"Charlotte."

Paul's eyes widened. "Charlotte of the field hospital?"

"Yes, Charlotte Zielinski."

His heart raced. "Yes, I know. Wait a minute. Charlotte said her brother was killed in battle."

"It was a mistake. I was captured, then I escaped seven months later. I'm very much alive because *you* saved my life."

The enormity of that statement didn't escape Paul. "What does Charlotte need?"

"They've recessed the hearing on Charlotte's and your character, because a man came forward to state that he and Charlotte...well, that they participated in immoral acts."

"What?" Paul spit as he yelled, "That's absurd."

"Of course, it is. But now there is doubt as to what happened in the basement of the *chateau,* and they need you to testify to her character and to what exactly happened between the two of you." He paused. "And, for some reason, Charlotte didn't attend the hearing, and we don't know where she is."

"What?" Paul grabbed onto Ian's arm.

"Sister Betty and the others are searching for her, but we have no idea where she is."

Paul gathered his belongings, along with the violin. "I'm ready to go whenever you are. And I think I know where she might be."

"You do?"

"Yes, but let's go quickly."

He stopped at the nurses' desk to inform them that he was releasing himself from the hospital.

The elderly sister behind the desk glared at him over her glasses. "What makes you think you can release yourself, Doctor?"

"I do. Thank you, Sister." He didn't wait to hear her response.

Outside, it was damp and misty, light fog covering the area.

Ian stared at the violin as they walked to the autocar. "That's..."

"Yes, Charlotte's violin." Paul hesitated.

"Charlotte's violin? The one Papa carved for her?"

"Yes. It was stolen by the Huns when we were in hiding at the *chateau*."

"It appears that I don't know the entire story."

"Either way, I bought it back for her. She was quite unhappy that it was stolen." He followed close behind Ian, then the two got into the autocar.

Ian started the car and turned onto a road barely visible through the fog. Speeding along, he seemed to drive by faith, not by sight.

Paul shifted on the seat but couldn't get comfortable. His head throbbed, and the wound in his back ached. Perhaps he should've taken an analgesic. He wanted to picture Charlotte smiling or laughing, but all he could see was her disappointed expression.

Ian's voice broke through the fog of Paul's mind. "You know my sister loves you."

Paul opened, then closed, his mouth. He cleared his voice. "Yes, yes, I know."

"Charli never told me once about her violin being gone, but I did hear about you."

"I see."

"If you've hurt my sister...."

"Ian, I don't intend to hurt your sister, at least not anymore. I intend to ask her to marry me."

Ian's shoulders relaxed. "Good. Because you will never meet a better girl than Charli. She can't play the violin

166

very well, but she is a fine young woman, generous to a fault, strong but sweet and kind."

"Charli? Cute. Anyway, I know, I know. You don't have to convince me any longer. It took another soldier's last words to make me see straight. And please don't say anything to Charlotte about the violin."

"Mum's the word, Doctor." Ian winked.

The two fell silent, and Paul stared ahead at the thick fog, its mystery giving him a sense of gloom. His heart skipped a beat. *Something has happened to her.*

"Can't you drive faster?"

"I *am* driving fast."

"Something's happened to your sister. I have a bad feeling."

Ian pressed his foot on the accelerator, and the two men flung back against the seat as the autocar sped across the road.

Chapter Thirty
Where is Charlotte?

When Charlotte hit bottom, she was stunned momentarily. A flash of pain seared the back of her head. She felt around but there was no blood, only a large goose-egg-sized bump. *I must've hit something on the way down.*

She blinked her eyes and attempted to assess her situation. A circle of daylight showed above her, about twenty feet up, but little light reached her down at the bottom of – where *was* she?

Reaching a hand out into the darkness, she touched a cold stone wall, the texture of it reminding her of the chapel walls. Using the wall to keep her balance, she climbed to her feet, but the dirt under her had too much give. Oh no! She was sinking into mud. *What is this place? An old well?*

She'd bumped her head and scraped and bruised herself all over, but as far she could tell, she had broken no bones.

Charlotte took a breath to calm herself, but a shiver ran through her. Glad she'd worn her shawl, she tightened it. So she'd fallen into a well. *Now what?*

Before she could answer her own question, her feet sank deeper into the mud below.

Would anyone even hear her pleas for help?

"Help!" she screamed in her loudest voice. Her voice ricocheted off the stone walls. She waited for a response. Nothing. Would she be able to hear anyone above her walking around?

***

The autocar pulled to a stop, and Sister Betty met the men. "Good to see you again, Dr. K. We haven't been able to find Charlotte. Some of our staff said they heard a distant explosion in the forest. It was probably another shell left over from the previous battle and only now detonated."

Paul didn't want to hear about any possible explosion. "I might know where she is. Ian, follow me!"

The two of them sprinted to the back of the *chateau*. Paul slowed his pace when he realized the fog was thicker closer to the forest.

"Why are we coming back here?" Ian asked.

"It's where we used to meet."

"I see."

Paul followed the long and winding path until they came to an area near the stone building. From the smoky scent, Paul surmised the shell had detonated close by.

His heart sank. Charlotte's missing. She should've been at the hearing. Scanning the area, he followed the scent until he came upon a still-smoking crater on the edge of the forest. *No sign of Charlotte here, thank God.* Slowly and carefully, the two men passed the stone building.

Turning, he swept the area with his gaze, then he studied the ground near the rear of the stone building. It appeared as if someone had taken some of the stones away from the back entrance. He poked his head inside, trying to allow his eyes to adjust to the darkness. Finally, he shook his head. She was not inside. But she *had* been here, he was certain of it.

***

Charlotte had screamed at the top of her lungs so many times that her voice was now hoarse, and she doubted she could yell anymore with any useful volume. Maybe if she gave her throat and voice a chance to rest, she could continue to scream for help. She rubbed her neck and shifted her body to find a more comfortable position. Her head throbbed, and the mud was now up to her shins.

***

Paul studied the ground searching for anything that might confirm that Charlotte had been here recently. The two men worked their way outward from the stone building. Ian shouted, "Charli!"

He followed Ian's voice through the fog until the young man came into view.

Ian stood with his mouth open and staring at something he held, a white scarf with a red dot on it.

As Paul raced forward, the red dot became a red cross. He drew in a breath.

Ian's lips pursed as he pointed downward to rotting wood that had been split open to reveal a large hole. "An old well! Dear God, she must've fallen in."

Paul's heart pounded.

Leaning over the hole, Ian shouted her name.

***

Charlotte straightened and lifted her chin as she heard the echoing sound "Charli" being called. "Yes!" she tried to scream, but her voice was hoarse. Ian was up there and would help her.

She tried to say, "Help me!" But all that came out was a hiss.

Charlotte swallowed a few times, clearing her throat and summoning every ounce of strength she could. Then she screamed, no words at all, just a scream. That's when she heard multiple voices above.

***

"Thank God!" Ian said. "We're going to get help, sis. Hang on!"

Releasing a sigh, Paul turned. Ian's face had more color to it now, and his eyes shone. The young man pressed a palm against his heart.

Paul squeezed his shoulder. "She's alive, she's communicating, and we're going to get her out. Now, we just have to figure out a way. Neither of us is strong enough to pull her out, given that we have had recent surgeries. Quickly follow the path back to the *chateau* and bring as many men and ropes as you can."

A look of determination on his face, Ian sprinted away.

When he left, Paul leaned over the hole. "Help is on the way, Charlotte!"

***

Charlotte listened and relaxed somewhat. She could hear the word "help" and "way." The rest of the words were garbled. Ian had found her, and she was going to be all right. Just then, the mud pulled her legs farther into oblivion.

***

It was only five minutes later, but as Paul watched the

minutes and seconds pass on his watch, it seemed an eternity. Ian, accompanied by three stretcher-bearers and another man dressed in civilian clothes came forward to assist.

"Over here, quick!"

Ian yelled down to Charlotte that they were throwing a rope down, but there was no response.

***

Charlotte was now immersed in mud right up to her mid thigh and wondering what she could do to keep from sinking deeper. Perhaps she could hang on to the rough point of a rock? As she was thinking, she heard Ian's voice. He said something about a rope. Before she could respond, something slapped down toward her, and she covered her head with her hands to protect herself. It bounced off her head, and she took hold of it. A rope!

"Tie it around yourself, Charli!"

She wrapped it around her body and under her arms. Charlotte yanked on the rope to indicate to Ian that she was ready to be hoisted out.

***

Paul watched as one of the men gripped the rope and another stood behind him. Yet another planted himself behind him, all men spaced about ten feet apart. The front man called out, "Watch her now. She might be hysterical when we get her out."

Ian laughed. "Charli? No way. She's definitely not the hysterical type, at least for most things."

Paul smiled to himself. Charlotte wasn't the hysterical type, not unless she's in the basement of a *chateau* during a siege.

It seemed that Charlotte had yanked on the rope, so the

three men began to pull her up. And they had pulled her nearly five feet when something went wrong.

***

Charlotte gasped in exasperation as the knot came undone and she slipped out of the line. She slid back into the muddy sludge at the bottom of the hole, the rope now out of her grasp. If she had been a swearing woman, she would've let out one big, bad word.

The men above were trying to help her. So, when the rope was tossed down again, she grasped hold of it, this time wrapping it around her upper body and under her arms twice. In the process, she pulled on the rope to get slack and the men above must've thought she was ready. When they started pulling upward, she snatched the rope back with all her might. She waited to make sure they understood that she was not ready.

Squeezing her eyes shut, she tried to remember how to tie a square knot. Ian had taught her years ago, and she furrowed her brow as she concentrated on making a proper knot. Once finished, she yanked on the rope again twice to indicate she was ready to be pulled up.

***

If Paul hadn't been so worried about Charlotte, he would've been smiling from ear to ear throughout the whole experience. Even from the bottom of a hole, Charlotte's personality shone through.

This time, the three men worked together to pull her up and out of the well. It was only when she was entirely out of the hole and lying on the ground that Paul allowed himself to breathe.

Even with her hair askew, mud covering most of the lower part of her body and her face splashed with dirt and mud, she was still the most beautiful girl in the world. He remained in the background to allow Ian to reach her first.

***

Strong hands under her arms lifted her up. Her brother Ian came in close to inspect her before she fully stood up. "Are you hurt, Charli?"

"No, just some scrapes and bruises. And a sizeable bump on the back of my head. I'll be fine. In no worse shape than when you used to beat me up." She slapped the side of his arm, then paused. "Did I miss the hearing?"

Ian laughed. "No. Well, you did, but – I'll explain later. Let's get you back to the *chateau* and the hearing."

When Charlotte turned to walk back to the *chateau*, she gasped. Paul stood only a few feet from her.

"Paul!" She cared not the least bit whether she would get him dirty or whether he would keep her at arm's distance. She was going to hug him whether he wanted it or not.

She raced to him and flung herself at him. He didn't step back, and he didn't push her away. "Oh, Paul. I'm so happy to see you."

"The feeling is reciprocal, my dear."

"You've come for the hearing?"

"Indeed I have." Paul winked, then smiled.

Too many thoughts were spinning inside her head. Paul was here! And he didn't try to stop her from hugging him. She tried not to get her hopes up too high, but she couldn't help it. His wink and smile made her swoon.

Chapter Thirty-One
Honor and Integrity Preserved

When Charlotte stepped into the dining hall for the hearing, a tall middle-aged man with an ugly moustache was on his way out the door. He did a double-take. She must have looked a sight since the bottom half of her skirt and shoes were still drenched in mud. Her hair fell in unruly tufts, mud streaked her face and arms, and her hands had never seen more dirt. She was filthy, but she had every intention of defending her character.

Lalonde gasped. A few others in the dining hall followed suit, then a loud hum floated throughout the crowd.

"I was about to leave, Miss Zielinski. I'm glad you made it in time. From the looks of it, you've been through quite an ordeal."

Charlotte opened her mouth to speak but her voice came out slow and raspy. "I'm... fine, sir... and want...to testify."

After she was sworn in, she sat in a chair beside the hearing officer's desk. Mud hardened like stone all over her, but she shook away the discomfort.

Paul took a seat beside Ian in the front row, and both men offered her encouraging smiles.

Monsieur Lalonde glanced at her. "Miss Zielinski, are you ready to answer a few questions?"

Clearing her throat again, she said, "Of course...please excuse my... appearance."

On the way back to the *chateau*, Ian had informed her as

to Cal's accusations. Charlotte couldn't believe Cal would lie. She tried explaining to Ian that it was probably payback because Charlotte wouldn't "have fun" with him. But that still didn't make much sense.

On the stand, she stated that she had only one interaction with Cal, and none of it entailed any sort of immoral behavior. She also testified that when she and Paul were in the basement during the siege, nothing licentious had occurred there either. She didn't lie; she was embarrassed and didn't want to offer up any information about the kiss. After all, a kiss wasn't licentious, was it? And hadn't they meant it to be private?

When Charlotte completed her testimony, Paul was then sworn in and Charlotte took the seat beside Ian. Charlotte looked down and followed the mud trail from the chair she had been sitting in to this chair. Before Paul sat down, he did nothing to clean the muddy mess she left on the chair. It was the first time Charlotte realized that he wasn't wearing his physician's coat.

Monsieur Lalonde said, "A previous witness has sworn that he and Miss Zielinski were involved in immoral behavior. And that you and Miss Zielinski were in the basement for three days and involved in immoral behavior. Would you like to comment on that, Doctor Kilgallen?"

"Yes, I certainly would. There is no finer young woman in the volunteer medical corps than Miss Charlotte Zielinski. She acted with honor, bravery, and selflessness when we were in the basement during the siege. There was no licentiousness nor was there any immoral behavior exhibited by her at any time, even in the several weeks after the siege. I would stake my military and medical career to say that anyone accusing her of immoral behavior is lying." He paused.

Charlotte nearly cried at his words.

"And might I add...."

"Yes?" asked Monsieur Lalonde.

"If anyone should be charged with possible immoral behavior, it should be me. While under siege in the basement of this *chateau*, Miss Zielinski and I kissed."

Monsieur Lalonde eyed Paul suspiciously.

Charlotte flung a hand to her chest and held her breath. *Dear God, what is he saying?*

"Or should I say, *I* kissed Miss Zielinski. And I can tell you from that one kiss, this girl has absolutely no experience with men. And I would never love or ask a worldly girl to marry me."

The hubbub in the room became louder with murmurs throughout the ever-growing crowd.

Charlotte's eyes widened, her mouth opened, and she finally exhaled. What had Paul just said? That he loved her? That he wanted to marry her? She was torn between shock and embarrassment and relief and excitement. Too many thoughts and emotions were spilling over to even comprehend.

"Thank you, Doctor. I'd like to have Private Harrison return for questioning." The now large crowd hummed and murmured.

Paul walked the short distance to where Charlotte and Ian were sitting. Ian got up so that Paul could sit next to Charlotte while they listened to Private Harrison's statement.

Charlotte could only stare forward, wide-eyed. Judging from the warmth of her cheeks, she was blushing. She still couldn't believe he had said the things he did. Could she be dreaming? This was too real to be a dream.

She avoided eye contact with him until he took her hand. Then she darted a glance. A smile playing on his lips, he brought her hand to his mouth and kissed it.

For a moment, everyone else in the room seemed to disappear. It was just the two of them.

Monsieur Lalonde's voice interrupted her thoughts. "After hearing Dr. Kilgallen's testimony, would you like to retract yours, Private Harrison?"

Cal sashayed forward as if he hadn't a care in the world. However, from where she sat in the front row, she could see that his forehead was beaded with sweat. He approached the chair, the mud still covering it, so he took out a handkerchief and cleaned it off.

His shoulders straightened, and he smirked. Then he rolled up his sleeves and pointed in a dramatic gesture towards Paul. He sputtered the words out, a sharp edge to his voice. "The good... doctor... he has a...well, uh... vested interest in this. He's, ye know, getting an award too." The corner of Cal's mouth lifted in a grin, and he pointed at Paul.

Charlotte stared at Cal's exposed right wrist as he pointed. Stunned, she grabbed Paul's arm.

Paul leaned in close. "What?"

"Tell them to stop."

"What?"

"Tell him we need a recess."

Paul stood. "Sir, may we please request a recess?"

Lalonde's eyebrows lifted. "Now? We just...."

"Yes. Miss Zielinski...." He glanced down at Charlotte.

"After the turmoil she's been through, she needs a glass of water. And, really, I should spend a few moments examining the injury to her head."

Monsieur's expression softened. "Yes, very well. I must make some notes anyway. We'll take fifteen minutes." He addressed Cal. "Please stay in the dining hall, sir."

Cal nodded.

Charlotte motioned to leave, but Paul held onto her arm. "Where are you going?"

"To the stone chapel."

"What chapel?"

"The stone chapel behind the *chateau* on the edge of the forest. Near where I was rescued."

"You mean the stone structure? Why do you call it a chapel?"

"Well, it has a cross, and it's stone. So, it's a stone chapel."

"Very well. I will come with you."

She first stopped at the entrance of the dining hall to get a glass of water. Then she raced – as fast as she could with the heavy weight of the mud-caked clothing, stockings and shoes – out the door, Paul at her side. Charlotte slowed when they neared the path along the edge of the forest as she thought she was going to faint.

"Are you all right?"

Nodding, she continued, but Paul held her back. "Let me check that bump on your head."

"Very well." She sighed and pointed.

He felt around for the bump. "Has it enlarged since the accident?"

"Not to my knowledge."

"You never lost consciousness when you fell?"

"No."

"And you haven't been sick to your stomach?"

"No."

"All right, then. Let's proceed."

The fog had finally lifted, but it was misty as they followed the path along the forest. The scent of fresh earth and grass permeated the air, but Charlotte couldn't revel in it. *I must get to the stone chapel!*

"Why are we going there?"

"You'll see."

When they arrived at the chapel, Charlotte first glanced toward the area of the old well from which she had earlier been rescued. The ropes, wood and stones lay scattered on the ground. She turned towards the stone chapel. Knowing she wouldn't have time to squeeze inside, she moved directly to the side wall, crouched down, wiggled a few stones until one came free.

She reached inside to the milk pail and felt around. There was a paper in the bucket, so she picked it up and pulled it outside. She unrolled it. This one had more writing than the letter she'd seen before. But this letter shared one very important similarity with the last letter: a coiled snake decorated the top of the page.

"What *is* this?" Paul asked.

"Long story. We need to get this paper back to the dining room." She stuffed it in her apron pocket.

"Let's go then." He took her hand, and they again sprinted on the path along the edge of the forest. Charlotte slowed.

"What?"

"I'm sorry, Paul. You're recuperating, and I'm running. Are you well enough to run?"

"I'm probably better able to run than you are after being pulled out of a well and having mud-drenched clothing."

"You have a point." The two quickened their pace as they left the path to return to the *chateau* and the dining hall.

Monsieur Lalonde glanced up as they entered the room. "Are you ready, Miss Zielinski?"

"Yes, sir, I am."

"Private Harrison, you may come back up here," Lalonde said.

Again, Cal strolled up to the front, his arms swaying back and forth. But now he seemed to be forcing a smile.

"May I approach Private Harrison?" Charlotte asked Lalonde.

He responded, "Yes."

With the note in her front pocket, she approached Cal. "Sir, might I see the inside of your right wrist?"

He shrugged and lifted his arm, revealing a long and coiled snake tattoo. Although he presented a confident front, his hand shook, and his face was beaded with perspiration.

"And do you know of the ancient stone structure in a clearing along the forest behind the *chateau*?"

"Of course, I do. You and I have been there many times." He leaned forward in the chair and chuckled nervously. "If you know what I mean." He ended the sentence with a pronounced smirk.

She wanted to wipe that smirk off his face. "Well, you

and I *have* both been there many times. But certainly not together."

"Come now, Charlotte, just admit it."

"I am mistaken. There *was* one time."

The assembly of people burst out in gasps and exclamations.

Cal cocked an eyebrow, then leaned forward.

She waited a few quiet seconds while Cal squirmed in his chair.

"Miss? Is this correct?" Lalonde questioned.

"Well...." She paused. "There *was* one time, but Private Harrison didn't know I was there." She reached into the pocket of her apron, took out the paper and held it in front of him. "Do you recognize this, Private Harrison?"

The man's face whitened. "Uh... I...uh... don't know what you mean. I don't know what that is."

"One day I was at the stone structure. I saw a man with a coiled snake tattoo on the inside of his wrist remove stones from the wall, then reach his hand into a milk pail hidden inside, pull a note out of it, then place another note into it."

Cal laughed nervously. "I don't know what you're talking about."

The buzz in the crowd grew ever louder.

Monsieur Lalonde said, "Shhh. Quiet!" Turning his attention to Charlotte, he said, "May I see the paper?"

"Of course." She handed it to him.

Lalonde held the paper up. "Private Harrison, have you any knowledge of this note?"

Cal stuttered and stammered. "For all I know, you placed that note in there, and you're now using it to make it seem like I'm a liar."

Sister Betty stood. "Might I interject, sir?'

"At this point, you might as well, Sister," said Monsieur Lalonde.

Charlotte faced Sister Betty and glimpsed Hannah near the doorway. The girl's face was scrunched up as if she had just eaten a sour lemon. This began to make sense. Cal and Hannah were an item. Perhaps Hannah asked him to do this? After all this time, Charlotte was hoping that Hannah had forgotten about her. That appeared not to be the case.

Charlotte turned her focus back to Sister Betty.

"Miss Zielinski came to me with the information that there might be someone in the *chateau* using the stone building as a hidden place to transport messages. I passed on that information to the authorities, but I don't believe anything has been done about it. However, I can attest to the fact that she did not fabricate this story."

Charlotte returned to the front row where Ian had saved another seat. She sat down.

Monsieur Lalonde nodded and wrote on the paper in front of him. "Well now, out of all the hearings I've held this year, this one has been the most entertaining."

He then turned his attention to Cal. "Young man, I'll leave it to the authorities of the Allied army to deal with you. But I find both Miss Zielinski and Dr. Kilgallen to be credible and of high character and honor. They are very much deserving of this award."

Glancing towards Charlotte and Paul, Monsieur said, "We shall see you in a few days. While I won't condone affection between professionals working together, I understand that the two of you were under much stress and perhaps facing death. I commend you both for your honesty, openness, and a courageous job well done."

"Thank you," Paul said, speaking on behalf of the two of them.

"This hearing is adjourned."

The dining hall became a flurry of activity with people talking and sharing their reactions. Charlotte blinked, and her ears began to ring.

From his chair beside her, Paul took her hand and pulled her into an embrace. "You, my dear, need to rest. Doctor's orders."

Ian handed her a glass of water, then patted her shoulder. "Charli, you may want to consider a career in law."

"Thank you for the water, but no thank you to the law career." She gulped it down and the coolness felt glorious on her throat.

"You haven't felt dizzy or nauseated?" Paul asked.

"Not until now, although I think it's because I'm exhausted."

"You probably have a slight concussion. Let me know if you have any headaches or dizziness."

"Of course."

Two British soldiers placed shackles on Private Harrison, then escorted him out, one on either side of him. "I'm innocent, I tell you. I'm not a spy. I'm not."

"If you lied about this young lady, what makes us think that you're not lying now?" Monsieur Lalonde asked.

When Paul wrapped his arms around her, she did what

she had been wanting to do since he left. She kissed his lips. It felt so natural, although they hadn't kissed in many months.

"What was that for?"

"My answer is yes."

"Yes what?"

"Yes, I'll marry you."

"You don't want to wait until I ask you?"

"I do not."

"And you don't need to think about it?"

"No."

"That's good, but we do need to discuss a few other items."

"Like what?"

Chapter Thirty-Two
Making Amends

Charlotte gingerly touched the back of her head.

Paul squeezed her shoulder. "We can discuss those issues tomorrow. You must get some rest."

"I'm fine, Paul, I just need to keep drinking water. But I would appreciate getting out of these muddy clothes and cleaning up. I must weigh a ton."

"Of course. I'll meet you in the foyer in about half an hour. I may just clean up myself."

Charlotte turned and weaved through the lingering crowd. She forced herself to walk as naturally as possible, despite the stiff, mud-caked clothes. It was evident wherever she went, she left a dirt-and-mud trail behind her.

In the dorm, she removed most of her garments and dropped them in a heap on the floor. She kept her slip on, put a towel over her arm and went to the women's bathroom. She turned on the water and put her hand under the lukewarm stream. Stepping into the tub, the cool temperature felt soothing. After soaking for a moment, she eased a dripping washcloth over her legs and arms using care over the scrapes and bruises. And no matter how much she rubbed, she couldn't clean every speck of mud and dirt. As she scrubbed, Charlotte thought about what Paul had said at the hearing.

Her life had certainly changed since this morning, when she had prayed to God to help her forget Paul. During one short day, Paul had proclaimed his love for her, and told the entire world of their first kiss and upcoming marriage.

She dressed in a clean skirt and blouse. Her arms and legs were still sore, but her heart was bursting at the news that they would be married.

Charlotte met Paul in the foyer. He wore a clean suit and tie. His eyes brightened when he saw her. "You're feeling well?"

"As well as can be expected."

He took her hand, and he accompanied her to the dining hall, now lit with electric lights. The room had been transformed back to a dining hall with tables and chairs set up for eating. Several patients and volunteers were scattered throughout the room. The people stared and smiled at them as they entered. Paul led her to the corner of the dining hall and to a table by the window, away from the others, that faced the exterior yard of the *chateau*.

So many questions raced through Charlotte's mind, but she waited. She wanted to tell him so many things. But she remained silent.

Paul held the chair out for her, and she lowered herself to the seat. "Wait here. I'll get some food for us."

He ventured over to the kitchen and picked up drinks and what looked like fresh bread and brought it back to the table. "I thought you might be hungry."

"I am."

He took the chair beside her.

She devoured one slice of warm bread, then drank the water to wash it down.

Paul sat with his eyes closed for a moment, as if trying to form words. Still, he said nothing. Patience was not

Charlotte's strongest virtue, and she opened her mouth to speak, "Paul –"

"Forgive me, Charlotte. I was so busy avoiding grief that I wasn't living. It took a dying soldier to make me realize that. And nearly getting blown to bits. Sister Aggie and Tom didn't make it."

"I'm so sorry." *Requiescant in pace, Sister Aggie and Tom.*

"I beg your forgiveness for not being more forthcoming with you in the weeks after the siege."

She wanted to drink in this beautiful moment to make up for all the times she felt lonely and forgotten. "Go on."

"And I beg your forgiveness for hurting you when I abruptly told you I was leaving."

She took hold of his hand. "You must know that I will forgive whatever you did. That's what it means to love, Paul."

Nodding, he continued. "I'm also sorry if I embarrassed you earlier, Charlotte. I hadn't intended on saying everything that I did. But since I mentioned our kiss, I needed to clarify it by saying I loved you and wanted to marry you."

"Charli!" The other people in the dining hall stared at Ian as he bounced through the large room toward her and Paul.

"Did you ask her yet?" Ian leaned his palms on their table, a big grin on his face and his eyes shifting from Paul to Charlotte.

Paul sat back and glanced toward the group at the nearest table, all of whom stared at the spectacle Ian had created. "Well, I already did in front of—"

"You mean your public marriage proposal?"

"She said yes."

Ian kissed his sister on the cheek. "The good doctor is smarter than I gave him credit for." Then he held out his hand to Paul. "Welcome to our little family, Doc."

Paul shook his hand. "Call me Paul, please. And welcome to my rather large family."

"Uh-oh. You have a large family?"

"Indeed. Eleven nieces and nephews, four sisters, all married."

"Well, Paul, Charli, it looks like we have some celebrating to do."

Charlotte waved her hand and stood up. "Perhaps tomorrow. I'm quite sore from today's events."

Paul also stood.

"I still can't believe everything that happened today."

Paul leaned in to kiss her cheek. "Then we'll talk about the date for our impending nuptials tomorrow."

"Of course. Goodnight, Paul." She turned toward her brother. "Goodnight, Ian."

***

Paul watched Charlotte retreat from the dining hall.

Ian patted him on the back.

"So, when is the happy occasion?"

"As soon as possible, if I have anything to say about it."

"Really? You mean you'll get married here in France?"

"That's my preference since my family will want to have a huge affair, and I'd rather avoid that and arrive home with my wife."

Chapter Thirty-Three
A Sacred Honor

Charlotte woke in a confused state. Did she dream all of this? Were she and Paul really getting married? When she sat up, pain shot through her body. Every bone, inch of skin and muscle groaned, and when she tried to stretch, her shoulders and legs objected the most. Her head throbbed, but the lump at the back of her head seemed smaller. Her body cried out in pain, but her heart sang with joy. It wasn't a dream.

She repositioned herself and stifled a groan to avoid disturbing anyone else in the dormitory. Balancing her bottom on the side of the bed, she took a couple of deep breaths. As she shrugged out of her nightgown, her gaze fell on the blue and yellow bruises and scrapes on her legs. No wonder she was in pain.

Of course, the joy in her heart was a soothing balm for any discomfort. She dressed as quickly as she was able.

In the hallway, she nearly ran into another girl.

Looking up, Hannah scowled. "You clumsy...."

A hint of irritation threatened Charlotte's joy but soon faded. She had an opportunity here. And Hannah had a genuine need.

"Hannah, you are correct. I am clumsy. I won't disagree with you there."

The girl scoffed.

"Hannah, I'm sorry you've had such a bad life. I'm sorry for whatever difficulties you're going through."

The girl lifted her chin. "I haven't had a difficult life."

"No?"

"No. It's been just fine."

"I know you were behind Cal's lies."

"Just trying to even up the score. Some girls get everything just handed to them."

Charlotte crossed her arms, breathed in deeply, then exhaled. This girl obviously had no idea about Charlotte's life. "Hannah, I lost my mother when I was six and my father, two and a half years ago. I have no idea what it's like to receive something I haven't worked for. Whatever you've had to endure in your life, I'm sorry. But I don't deserve your anger or your envy or whatever you have against me."

She didn't wait to hear Hannah's response and made her way to Paul's room in the west wing. At his door, she held out her hand to knock, then pulled it back. Paul needed as much rest as she did, so she decided not to bother him.

Downstairs, Ian met her in the foyer. "I've been waiting for you for an hour, sis. They want to ship me back stateside after the award ceremony next week, but I was hoping to stay for the wedding, if it's soon. I'd like to bring Zélie along."

"That would be wonderful, Ian. But I have no idea when we'll get married. The sooner, the better."

Charlotte gave her brother the tightest hug possible, then went straight to the smaller barrack that housed four critically ill men. Since there were only four terminal men left, no nurse or aides were assigned to the ward full-time. Various sisters and volunteers checked on the men once or twice an hour. However, Charlotte tried her best to be there as much as possible.

Of the four remaining men, one was an American boy, a "basket case" who was still hanging on despite a deadly infection. He had only gained consciousness once or twice while she was present.

The other three men were British. Two of them were unconscious, but one British soldier stared at her as she approached his cot. He had been brought in a few days ago, and she had spent some time reading to him. Corporal Robert Jenson was a handsome man with dark hair, dark eyes, and a ruddy complexion and likely had a sweetheart back in England.

First, she searched for a chair to place beside the man's cot, but it appeared that all the chairs had been removed from this ward, perhaps for the hearing yesterday? She picked up a short wooden stool and decided this would have to do.

"Hello, Corporal. Would you like me to read to you or write a letter to someone back home?"

He said nothing. Instead, he forced a smile and held his hand up to her.

She gently took hold of his hand. As she adjusted herself on the stool, she groaned, and the British chap's eyes widened.

He squeezed her hand – as hard as his weak body could – and frowned.

Charlotte responded, "Don't worry about me. Just sore from falling into an old well yesterday. I'll be fine. In fact, I'll be *more* than fine."

Corporal Jenson nodded, then relaxed against his pillow. His breathing was labored, and at times, he squeezed her hand.

Charlotte leaned her head against the side of the cot and found herself nodding off.

A man behind her cleared his throat, startling her.

Opening her eyes, she looked up, joy filling her heart.

Paul stood behind her and opened his mouth to speak. Not wanting his voice to wake Corporal Jenson, she put her finger to her lips.

She gently released the corporal's hand and placed it on the cot.

They walked together to the doorway. He whispered, "You must be hungry. Ian tells me you've been here for four hours."

"Four hours!" she whisper-shouted. Lowering her voice, she said, "I can't believe I've been here that long. Yes, I'm very hungry. But I don't want to leave Corporal Jenson."

"I'll bring you something to eat and wait with you."

"That would be wonderful."

***

Paul carried a tray of food to the barrack, anxious to return to Charlotte. After falling in the well, she must've been in a great deal of discomfort, despite no obvious broken bones or sprains. Yet, she sacrificed herself to stay with a dying man. *She's one very special girl.*

He hoped he could convince her to have the wedding next week, after the awards ceremony. It was quick, yes, but if his family got a hold of the wedding planning, it would be the grandest affair in the Ottawa Valley. He didn't want that, although if Charlotte desired an elaborate affair, he would acquiesce to her wishes.

***

Charlotte hummed quietly because she didn't want to

wake the other men in the ward. Then she whispered prayers for Corporal Jenson. A single electric lamp glowed near the desk, casting dim light and a somber mood in the ward. Leaning close to the man's ears, she whispered, "Sir, you are loved, by your family, by God, and by me."

He blinked then opened his eyes. His gaze pierced her heart and soul. One solitary tear had started its way down his cheek.

"Oh my." She wiped it away with her thumb. "Corporal, you are loved."

He squeezed her hand once, then he began to thrash about in the bed.

"Oh no!" She tried to hold on firmly to his hand, but he was stronger than she was, and it flipped out of her grasp. She hummed quietly to him, and he relaxed against the bed.

He opened his mouth, as if attempting to take another breath, grunted, then was still, his eyes and mouth open.

"Sir? Corporal?"

No response. She gently lifted his wrist and felt for a pulse. None. *Requiescat in pace.* "Eternal rest grant unto him, O Lord, and let perpetual light shine upon him. And may his soul and all the souls of the faithful departed, through the mercy of God, rest in peace. Amen."

Another name to be added to my book of the dead. Charlotte's eyes filled with tears. Sorrow overwhelmed her, and she squeezed her eyes shut to keep the tears from coming. She wished that she could have done more for this man.

Scanning the three remaining men, she realized that soon the war would be over, and she would be leaving France, and her job here would be finished. She had been present at the bedside of hundreds of dying soldiers and not one survived. Charlotte tried to picture each one of them in her mind and the bond they shared. As feeble and as non-present as many of them were, she missed each one and continued to pray for them.

William, the first soldier she sang into eternity, was a kind boy who had suffered so much. There was Sergeant Kennedy and just now, Corporal Jenson. All these beautiful souls...before the war, they were living, laughing, loving. And now? They were gone.

Drawing in a breath, she sat straight in her chair. Her faith assured her they were on the way to – or already in – heaven. They had died, but their souls lived on.

The kindness that I was able to give those men, whatever I was able to do to lessen their fears and anxieties, the soothing words, the soft singing, the prayers, will live on with them in eternity. I hope that I've been able to assure them that they were loved and that they would be going to a beautiful place where there was no more pain or suffering.

Each of these men deserved their last moments to be as honorable, as positive, as pleasant, warm and loving as possible. If she had not been there with them, each of their deaths would have been different. She couldn't stop their deaths just like she couldn't stop her parents' deaths. She couldn't even stop their pain. But Charlotte was able to turn every one of those moments into love, a reflection of God's abundant grace for each one of them.

And not just for them, but for her. She had received so much from each of these men. It had been a sacred honor and privilege to be present with each one of them as they passed from this life.

She squeezed Corporal Jenson's hand one last time, closed his eyes and mouth, then kissed the top of his head. She covered his body with a linen sheet. Near the door, she searched for Corporal Jenson's file to indicate the hour of death, 18:20 hours.

With this newfound revelation, Charlotte made another decision. She would remain in this barrack until the last man had passed away, even if it meant she had to stay twenty-four hours per day.

She returned the file to the desk, then made her way to each of the three other soldiers. All seemed to be sleeping peacefully under the influence of morphine.

The barrack door opened behind her. Paul came in with a bowl of what looked like soup or stew.

She walked toward him. "Thank you." She took the food from him and sat at the desk near the door. "Corporal Jenson passed peacefully a few moments ago."

"I see." Paul cocked his head. "Why are you smiling?"

"I've had a bit of a revelation. I'll tell you about it later."

"Of course. I hope you like this stew."

"As Papa used to say, if it isn't moving, I'll like it. Right now, I like anything."

Paul laughed. "There's so much I need to learn about you, Charlotte." He paused as she bowed her head to say a short prayer before eating.

She blessed herself. "That can be said for both of us."

"Or should I call you Charli?" He chuckled.

She dipped the spoon in the stew and held it to her mouth. It smelled of rosemary, savory and parsley. "You may call me whatever you'd like." She swallowed a spoonful of food.

"I prefer Charlotte. Charlie is the name of my father's butcher. So...when and where do you want to get married? Do you want a big wedding or a small one?"

Charlotte gulped down another mouthful of stew before answering. "Without sounding too impatient, anytime in the next week or so would be wonderful."

"Perfect."

"Perfect?"

"Yes. Now the other question. A large affair or a small one?"

"I would think you would know the answer to that one. I only have my brother and, of course, a few of my friends here, so small, please."

***

Paul blew out a sigh of relief. "I'm definitely marrying the right girl."

"Oh?"

"I prefer that we marry here, maybe even next week after the awards ceremony. Then your brother and sister-in-law can attend, as well as any friends you think would be able to come." Paul hesitated, curious as to why Charlotte had a permanent smile plastered to her lovely face. "What is this realization you've had?"

After sharing her revelation, she said, "There are only three dying men remaining, and I wish to stay with them night and day so that I'm with them when they pass into eternity."

"I understand."

"You don't mind?"

"Of course not."

Charlotte finished eating another spoonful of stew.

"Tomorrow, I'm going with some of the men to the stone building to make sure the well is covered. No need for anyone else to fall in."

Charlotte stopped eating and her face brightened. "That would be perfect, Paul!"

"What would be perfect?"

"The stone chapel. We can be married by the stone chapel!"

"That all depends on the weather. If it's raining or snowing, not likely."

"Please! It's the ideal place."

"Let's see if we can first find a Catholic priest to perform the wedding." He hesitated. "And I suppose I will need to go to confession. I owe it to God after ignoring him for so many months, and I haven't been to Mass since university."

"Then that same priest can hear your confession."

***

Hannah hated the death ward, but Sister Betty only asked her to check on the men, and that's all she planned to do. She despised being near death, which is why she avoided that ward, if possible.

She was about to open the door of the death barrack when she heard Charlotte speaking to Dr. Tall and Handsome. She had been angry that they were getting married.

After Charlotte spoke with her in the hallway earlier that day, she realized that she and Charlotte had a lot more in common than she had originally thought.

Hannah had also lost both her parents, her mother when she was four and her father when she was fifteen. But as she listened to Charlotte go on and on about what an honor it was to be with dying men, Hannah's heart softened. She shouldn't have encouraged Cal to malign Charlotte. Maybe she should just let bygones be bygones.

Chapter Thirty-Four
Wedding at the Stone Chapel

Four days later, Charlotte stayed at the bedside of the last remaining terminal soldier, the "basket case," a young American private by the name of Seth Golder. He was called a "basket case" because he had lost both arms and legs in an explosion near the front and was carried off in a basket. With closed eyes and barely stirring, he seemed at peace. Every now and then, when he took a deep breath, light caught on the Jewish Star of David that he wore on a silver chain around his neck.

It was a shame this young man was injured and would die so close to the end of the war. But the doctors could do little to help because infection had already ravaged what was left of his body. He was now in septic shock. She had stayed with him for over twenty-four hours, calming him when he occasionally opened his eyes.

Charlotte nodded off here and there on a cot nearby determined to stay with him until his time came, even if it meant moving the wedding to the death ward beside the private's bed.

After resting for a short time, her eyes flew open at the sound of a man's voice.

"H...help."

"Of course," she said, leaning close to him, looking into his eyes, though his lids hung at half-mast. "What can I do for you, Private Golder?"

He used his chin to indicate the Star of David. "Star...please send... to my parents."

"Yes, yes, I will. I promise. Is there anything else you'd like me to tell them?"

He closed his eyes, and she rested her hand on his chest. "I'm here. You are loved, sir. I am here."

He swallowed. "Don't tell...."

"Don't tell what?"

"Parents, about...."

"About?"

"No legs...arms."

"Oh, sir. You are still as whole as you've ever been."

"Tell them...I love them."

"Of course. I'll tell them you love them."

"Thank...you."

"Thank *you*, Private." She kept her hand on his chest as his entire body seemed to relax. He was gone. "Eternal rest, grant unto him...." *Rest in peace, Private Seth Golder.*

***

The next day at the French Legion Awards ceremony, Paul and Charlotte were presented with their awards before a cozy group of comrades. Charlotte was surprised at how heavy the medal was. When the man pinned it to her apron, she almost toppled over.

After the ceremony and accompanying luncheon, while most of the medical staff and patients were celebrating the official end of the war, Paul and Charlotte prepared to be wed by a local parish priest, Père Charles Mercier, who had expressed delight in being able to perform a wedding ceremony amidst the war-ravaged *chateau*. He was a tall, slender man who spoke English impeccably and, for that, Charlotte was appreciative.

A cool breeze blew, but fortunately, they had neither rain nor snow, so they could be married at the stone chapel.

Charlotte was disappointed that her friend Julia had recently left to join her fiancé in Le Treport, France, and wouldn't be able to attend. However, she understood. Had she given her friend more than a few days' notice, Julia would have been able to attend.

Her uniform and apron had been freshly washed and pressed for the occasion. Charlotte could've bought a dress, but since Paul would be wearing his Army uniform, she would wear her blue and white uniform as well.

In front of the *chateau*, a group of medical volunteers had congregated nearby, as well as some of the healthier patients. Charlotte was happy that so many of her fellow volunteers and nurses wanted to witness their wedding.

As she scanned the group, her eyes came upon Hannah Greene, and she blew out a breath. What was *she* doing here? When Hannah saw that she was looking at her, she glanced away. Charlotte stared until Hannah made eye contact again. Was that the slightest of smiles on the girl's face?

The priest arrived, and Charlotte welcomed him, then checked the timepiece on her apron. It was already two minutes to the wedding, but she had no idea where Paul was. They were supposed to be at the stone chapel by 14:00 hours. "Where is Paul?"

Ian leaned in close. "Don't worry. I think he's already there."

"Then we should make our way back there."

When the large group had walked about halfway down the path, Ian took off in a sprint, saying, "Wait here. I'll be right back."

They all stopped. Charlotte scowled and cocked her head. "What's going on?"

The priest's eyebrows lifted, and he grinned. Sister Betty and Zélie also smiled.

When Ian returned, he was out of breath. "Everything is ready."

"Is it now?"

"Yes, Charli, it is."

Once they reached a copse of trees on the edge of the forest and close to the stone chapel, Ian urged the priest, Sister Betty, Zélie, and the entire group of medical volunteers and patients to go on ahead of them.

"What are you doing, Ian?"

"I'm giving my dearest sister away at her wedding."

Charlotte leaned up to kiss his cheek, then took hold of his arm. "How do we know when to walk up to the –"

Music – beautiful, sweet, flawless violin music – floated through the air. *Paul. Playing the violin.* She recognized the melody as "Somewhere a Voice is Calling," one of the first songs he had taught her to sing.

With Charlotte grasping onto his arm, Ian briskly walked. They came around the copse of trees.

In front of the old stone chapel stood the priest, his vestments blowing in a gentle breeze, and Paul, so handsome in his uniform and especially as he played the violin. She focused on his intense dark eyes.

When they reached the stone chapel, Paul finished the

last few notes, then leaned the instrument against the wall. He joined Ian and Charlotte in front of the priest. Ian kissed his sister's cheek and gave her hand to Paul.

Paul's face shone with happiness. But there was also a twinkle in his eye.

Zélie stood in as Charlotte's matron of honor. As well as giving his sister away in marriage, Ian was also Paul's best man.

Much of the ceremony was in Latin, but when it came to the vows, they were in English.

"Paul Alistair Kilgallen, wilt thou take Charlotte Patricia Zielinski to be thy lawful wedded wife, to have and to hold, for richer, for poorer, in sickness and in health, till death do thou part?"

Paul answered, "Yes, I will."

Charlotte closed her eyes and savored his words like fine chocolate.

The priest cleared his throat. "Charlotte Patricia Zielinski, wilt thou take Paul Alistair Kilgallen to be thy lawful wedded husband, to have and to hold, for richer, for poorer, in sickness and in health, till death do thou part?"

"I will." Her heart filled with joy.

The priest sprinkled holy water on the rings and recited more Latin.

Paul placed the ring on her finger and repeated prayers, which Father had recited, then Charlotte did the same.

"Ego conjungo vos in matrimonium in Nomine Patris et Filii et Spiritus Sancti, Amen." They all made the sign of the cross.

"Congratulations, Doctor and Mrs. Kilgallen. You may kiss your bride."

Paul leaned down and kissed Charlotte gently on the lips. Everyone behind them clapped. Paul shook the priest's hand. "Thank you, Father. Thank you for taking time out of your day to marry us."

"I did not marry you. I am just the officiant. The bride and groom marry each other."

"Well, thank you very much."

"My pleasure. Now, I have your marriage certificate prepared, and if your two witnesses and everyone else will accompany me back to the *chateau* to sign the official register, we'll allow the two of you to have a private moment."

Everyone ambled away until no one remained except Paul and Charlotte.

"Dr. Kilgallen, what on earth are you hiding from me?"

"The most extraordinary gift in the world."

"What gift?"

"Close your eyes."

"Very well." She squeezed her eyes shut. She couldn't even begin to imagine what sort of gift he had for her. In fact, Paul was the best gift she could ever receive.

"Are you ready?"

"Yes." As she slowly opened her eyes, her gaze fell on a violin he held. He turned it around to show her the back of it. Her eyes widened, and her mouth fell open as she studied the ornate carvings. "It's...it's the – "

"It certainly is."

"— violin Papa carved for me! What a beautiful gift! How did you find it? *Where* did you find it?"

"It's a long story that I'll save for later. There's quite a crowd waiting for us in the dining hall."

***

After an hour or so of celebrating, Paul and Charlotte bid farewell to Ian and Zélie. Charlotte assured them that they would be in the States before Christmas.

The priest approached them to say his farewell. "Congratulations, Doctor and Mrs. Kilgallen."

"Thank you, Father," Charlotte said, not yet accustomed to hearing the name "Mrs. Kilgallen."

"By the way," he said, "do you know the history of that little stone building where we performed the wedding?"

Both Paul and Charlotte shook their heads.

"It is common knowledge in this part of the country that Saint Colette of Corbie stopped at the house that used to be adjacent to the stone building on her way to Nice to visit the pope. The mother of the house was in labor when she arrived, but it became apparent that both the woman and her baby would not survive. Saint Colette asked if there was a quiet place she could pray, and the woman's husband escorted her to the stone building. She remained there for hours until the baby was born, and both mother and baby survived. It's one of two miracles that are attributed to her intercession."

Charlotte opened her mouth, surprised.

Paul nodded. "You were right, Charlotte. It *is* a holy building."

"In addition," the priest said, "after Saint Colette left, the man put the cross on the stone shed in thanksgiving for his wife and newborn daughter." He paused. "Their daughter eventually joined Saint Colette's order of sisters."

"Thank you for sharing that beautiful story. Now I

understand why I felt it was such a sacred place."

"Interestingly, the stone building has remained, but the house was destroyed in a fire over a hundred years ago."

***

Since Paul was still recuperating from his injury and Charlotte was sore from her fall-down-the-well experience, the two retired early to a private room in the west wing of the *chateau*.

With all that had happened in such a short time, Charlotte hadn't thought much about what was about to take place. She was nervous, but she loved Paul with her heart, her soul, and her mind. She would now love Paul with her body.

She took Paul's hand, then knelt beside the bed. "Dear Father in Heaven, please bless our marriage."

The two shall become one.

***

Upon waking, Charlotte was filled with abundant joy. Paul was now her husband, and they would start their life together right here in France.

In the ensuing weeks, Paul accepted a full-time surgical position at the Hotel Dieu Hospital in Kingston, Ontario, his hometown. She was about to write to Ian, when she received a letter from him the beginning of December telling her that he had found a job in Watertown, New York, close to the Canadian/US border. Without having a map in front of her, she asked Paul how close Watertown, New York, was to Kingston. He let out a hearty laugh. "An hour's train ride."

Charlotte squealed. "Do you mean to say that we will be only an hour from my brother and his wife?"

"Yes."

Chapter Thirty-Five
Christmas in Canada

Charlotte and Paul stepped off the boat in New York Harbor. It was a chilly December day the week before Christmas. They then took the train to New Jersey to pick up Charlotte's trunk of possessions that she had left at the rectory for safekeeping. She introduced Paul to Fr. Kowalski, but they soon bid farewell.

Then they took the train to Watertown, New York, to surprise Ian and Zélie and their newborn son, Joseph Karl. After spending three days with them, they boarded another train to Ottawa, Ontario, to spend the holidays with Paul's large extended family.

When Paul told Charlotte that his family was loud, boisterous and didn't take no for an answer, Charlotte assumed he might be exaggerating.

The entire family met the couple at the train station in Ottawa. In fact, it seemed like the entire city of Ottawa had met them.

Charlotte was first introduced to Mr. and Mrs. Kilgallen. They were a striking couple. Mr. Kilgallen, although only forty-eight, was totally gray, tall, and broad-shouldered. Paul obviously inherited his handsome looks from his father. Mrs. Kilgallen was a shorter woman with a sprinkling of gray in brown hair pulled up in a chignon. She wore a stunning gray-blue day dress. She chattered on non-stop about how worried she had been for her only son, and she was so happy he had found a new wife and only wished they were going to live in Ottawa instead of Kingston.

Four women and their husbands were introduced one by one to Charlotte, but after the past year in Europe, she was overwhelmed and would not likely remember any of their names. The young ladies all chatted non-stop. Paul stayed close by, seemingly to ensure no one monopolized her time.

It was only when Charlotte visited the family home that she realized Paul's family was more than "well-to-do." The home in the Rockcliffe Manor section of Ottawa was nothing short of a mansion. They entered the foyer and were greeted by two maids and one butler and many children ranging in ages, it seemed, between one and ten. A large balsam fir at least ten feet high and decorated with balls, tinsel and electric lights stood majestically in the left corner of the foyer, with more gifts than Charlotte had seen in her entire life.

She turned to Paul. "You didn't say you were *this* wealthy."

"I told you that we are a family of means."

"A bit of an understatement, dear husband."

"Paul, Charlotte," Mrs. Kilgallen said, "you'll be staying in the spare bedroom on the third floor. Everyone else will be staying on the second floor. That way, you'll have privacy and you'll have your own washroom, as well."

***

Christmas Eve arrived the following day, and the family attended Midnight Mass at St. Patrick's Cathedral in downtown Ottawa, filling three entire pews. The choir's exquisite music echoed through the church. The irony didn't escape Charlotte. One year ago, she had attended Mass on Christmas Day, believing she had no relatives left.

This year, her brother was alive, married, and was a father. And she was part of this substantial family.

A wave of nausea struck her, making her sway to one side.

Paul wrapped his arm around her and pulled her to his side. "You all right?"

She grabbed the back of the pew and nodded, smiling to assure him that she was fine, though she hadn't felt well lately.

When they returned home, everyone went to their respective bedrooms with the promise that gifts would be opened in the morning.

Charlotte and Paul retired as well, but Charlotte didn't want to sleep until she gave Paul his Christmas gift. She had gotten the idea from her friend Julia, who had bought gifts for her future beloved even before she met him. When she found this particular item in her trunk, she was convinced it was tailor-made for Paul.

"Paul?"

"Yes, love?"

"I'd like to give you my gift now. Is that all right?"

"Of course."

Charlotte reached into her luggage and pulled out a very flat package, already gift-wrapped in bright red paper. "I hope you like this."

***

Paul took the gift from his wife and cocked his head. "It's light enough to be paper."

"Open it, Paul."

He ripped open the package to find a large brown envelope. He pulled out several pieces of paper – it was sheet music – and when he saw the title, he laughed out loud.

"Shh, Paul."

"Sorry, but this is perfect."

"It's one of the very first editions from 1835."

"I shall treasure it always." He read the title. "'Home, Sweet Home.' Just perfect."

"That's not all, dear husband."

"Oh?"

"See if you can find little Charlotte's gift to you."

"Little Charlotte?" His eyes narrowed, and he studied the sheet music for – and there it was. On the bottom of one of the pages, a child – Charlotte at a younger age – had drawn stick figures of what appeared to be a man and a woman. And under it, "Charli."

"Papa wasn't too pleased that I had used his sheet music to draw. I don't remember doing this, but I do remember always doodling two people, and Ian saying, 'I'm not bigger than you, Charli,' because at that age, he wasn't. So, I'm convinced that it was you I had been drawing all along."

"Well, dear wife, this is absolutely the most exquisite gift I shall ever receive." He kissed the top of her head.

Charlotte stepped back. "Even though it's one of the first editions, it's probably not worth much monetarily. My doodle ruined that."

"Ah, but the doodle – it's priceless."

Epilogue
And Baby Makes Three

October 4, 1919

Charlotte peered out the window of their home facing Lake Ontario in Kingston. She would never tire of the beautiful sunrises she was treated to most mornings. The leaves, which had already begun to turn vibrant shades of orange, yellow, and red created a breathtaking view.

Her memories of the first few months of this year were hazy at best. She had an extreme case of all-day sickness because she had been with child.

Paul had been ecstatic about the news.

With each passing day since leaving Europe, the war was that much further behind them. She kept the journal of the dead in her nightstand and continued to pray for their souls. She occasionally received a letter of gratitude from the parents or wife of one of the soldiers from the death ward.

The most notable and best distraction from any painful memories of war was their new daughter, Colette Marie Kilgallen, born September 8.

Since their daughter had been conceived in Europe, Charlotte and Paul chose a name that was indicative of their time in France.

Although Paul had been working long hours at the hospital, he came home every evening to hold and admire their baby girl.

Today would be Colette's christening, to be held at St.

Mary's Cathedral in Kingston. Paul had left to pick up Ian and Zélie – who would stand in as Colette's godparents – and in a few hours, the entire Kilgallen clan would be arriving in five autocars.

A year ago, she and Paul were in France, Paul at the front and she at the field hospital. So much had happened in that one short year. She still had to pinch herself to believe that she was married to Paul and that Paul loved her. Whenever Paul held their daughter and cooed to her or made funny faces, she fell more in love with him.

Baby Colette whimpered in her cradle and Charlotte picked her up. The door opened, and Paul greeted them. "How are my two best girls?" He kissed Charlotte, then kissed the top of the baby's head.

"Your two best girls are doing well, thank you."

"Ian, Zélie, and Joseph are downstairs in the parlor. Mrs. Gleason is getting them some tea and cakes."

"I need to feed the baby first. But I should be done shortly."

"I'll let them know."

When Paul left, Charlotte sat in the rocking chair, unbuttoned her blouse, and began to nurse the baby. As her daughter sucked and swallowed, her little eyes rolled to the top of her lids as if she had been given a drug to ease her pain.

It brought Charlotte back to France and to the cellar of the *chateau* and to the death ward and the stone chapel. It had been an awful war that claimed too many young lives. Charlotte singing to and holding hundreds of men's hands as they passed into eternity had been the greatest honor of the war.

The Great War also brought this "great love" to her. And

she would spend her lifetime thanking God for Paul and now for Colette.

The baby stopped nursing and sighed as if in appreciation. Charlotte had never heard any sound so sweet.

Book 1 Julia's Gifts is available now.

Book 3, Ella's Promise,

will be available in November of 2019.

Acknowledgements

Special thanks to the Arnprior and District Museum (Cathy Rodger) for lending us the vintage clothes to photograph the cover. Thank you also to Mallory Brumm for posing for the cover.

Thank you to Theresa Linden for the excellent job of copyediting. This book would not be nearly as polished without your keen eye. To Dr. Jean Egolf, for reading through the manuscript and making sure medical terms and procedures were correct. To Ann Frailey for going above and beyond the job of proofreader! To Nick Lauer, Sarah Loten, and Carolyn Astfalk for proofreading and helpful editing advice.

My gratitude to Ian Frailey for coming up with the series title: Great War Great Love. The character of Ian Zielinski was named after you!

It's hard to convey my gratitude to my incredibly talented husband, James, in a few short sentences. This book truly would not exist without your assistance. Special thanks for listening patiently as I shared plot lines and character studies and received valuable feedback.

About the Author

Ellen Gable (Hrkach) is an award-winning author (2010 IPPY Gold, 2015 IAN finalist), publisher (2016 CALA), editor (2016 CALA), self-publishing book coach, speaker, NFP teacher, Marriage Preparation Instructor, Theology of the Body teacher, and past president of the Catholic Writers Guild. She is an author of nine books and a contributor to numerous others. Her novels have been collectively downloaded over 680,000 times on Kindle. She and her husband, James, are the parents of five adult sons and seven precious souls in heaven. In her spare time, Ellen enjoys reading on her Kindle, researching her family tree, and watching classic movies and TV shows. Her website is located at http://www.ellengable.com.

Ellen enjoys receiving feedback from her readers: please email her at fullquiverpublishing@gmail.com

Published by
Full Quiver Publishing
PO Box 244
Pakenham ON K0A2X0
Canada
http://www.fullquiverpublishing.com/

Made in United States
North Haven, CT
17 February 2022

16202238R00131